*This novel is for the Montana Gang.*

TOUCHSTONE

# The Hawkline Monster
## *A Gothic Western*

## Richard Brautigan

*A Touchstone Book*
*Published by Simon and Schuster*

A Touchstone Book
Published by Simon and Schuster
Rockefeller Center, 630 Fifth Avenue
New York, New York 10020

Designed by Elizabeth Woll
Manufactured in the United States of America

1   2   3   4   5   6   7   8   9   10

Library of Congress Cataloging in Publication Data

Brautigan, Richard.
The Hawkline monster; a gothic western.

I. Title.
PZ4.B826Haw [PS3503.R2736]   813'.5'4   74-6204
ISBN: 0-671-21809-3

ISBN 0-671-22156-6 pbk.

*The author and publisher wish to thank
the Edward B. Marks Music Corporation
for permission to reprint material from
"Bill Bailey, Won't You Please Come Home?"
© copyright Edward B. Marks Music Corporation.*

# Book 1

## · Hawaii ·

# · The Riding Lesson ·

They crouched with their rifles in the pineapple field, watching a man teach his son how to ride a horse. It was the summer of 1902 in Hawaii.

They hadn't said anything for a long time. They just crouched there watching the man and the boy and the horse. What they saw did not make them happy.

"I can't do it," Greer said.

"It's a bastard all right," Cameron said.

"I can't shoot a man when he's teaching his kid how to ride a horse," Greer said. "I'm not made that way."

Greer and Cameron were not at home in the pineapple field. They looked out of place in Hawaii. They were both dressed in cowboy clothes, clothes that belonged to Eastern Oregon.

Greer had his favorite gun: a 30:40 Krag, and Cameron had a 25:35 Winchester. Greer liked to kid Cameron about his gun. Greer always used to say, "Why do you keep that rabbit rifle around when you can get a real gun like this Krag here?"

They stared intently at the riding lesson.

"Well, there goes 1,000 dollars apiece," Cameron said. "And that God-damn trip on that God-damn boat was for nothing. I thought I was going to puke forever and now I'm going to have to do it all over again with only the change in my pockets."

Greer nodded.

The voyage from San Francisco to Hawaii had been the most terrifying experience Greer and Cameron had ever gone through, even more terrible than the time they shot a deputy sheriff in Idaho ten times and he wouldn't die and Greer finally had to say to the deputy sheriff, "Please die because we don't want to shoot you again." And the deputy sheriff had said, "OK, I'll die, but don't shoot me again."

"We won't shoot you again," Cameron had said.

"OK, I'm dead," and he was.

The man and the boy and the horse were in the front yard of a big white house shaded by coconut trees. It was like a shining island in the pineapple fields. There was piano music coming from the house. It drifted lazily across the warm afternoon.

Then a woman came out onto the front porch. She carried herself like a wife and a mother. She was wearing a long white dress with a high starched collar. "Dinner's ready!" she yelled. "Come and get it, you cowboys!"

"God-damn!" Cameron said. "It's sure as hell gone now. 1,000 dollars. By all rights, he should be dead and halfway through being laid out in the front parlor, but there he goes into the house to have some lunch."

"Let's get off this God-damn Hawaii," Greer said.

# · Back to San Francisco ·

Cameron was a counter. He vomited nineteen times to San Francisco. He liked to count everything that he did. This had made Greer a little nervous when he first met up with Cameron years ago, but he'd gotten used to it by now. He had to or it might have driven him crazy.

People would sometimes wonder what Cameron was doing and Greer would say, "He's counting something," and people would ask, "What's he counting?" and Greer would say, "What difference does it make?" and the people would say, "Oh."

People usually wouldn't go into it any further because Greer and Cameron were very self-assured in that big relaxed casual kind of way that makes people nervous.

Greer and Cameron had an aura about them that they could handle any situation that came up with a minimum amount of effort resulting in a maximum amount of effect.

They did not look tough or mean. They looked like a relaxed essence distilled from these two qualities. They acted as if they were very intimate with something going on that nobody else could see.

In other words, they had the goods. You didn't want to fuck with them, even if Cameron was always counting things and he counted nineteen vomits back to San Francisco. Their living was killing people.

And one time during the voyage, Greer asked, "How many times is that?"

And Cameron said, "12."

"How many times coming over?"

"20."

"How's it working out?" Greer said.

"About even."

# · Miss Hawkline ·

Even now Miss Hawkline waited for them in that huge very cold yellow house . . . in Eastern Oregon . . . as they were picking up some travelling money in San Francisco's Chinatown by killing a Chinaman that a bunch of other Chinamen thought needed killing.

He was a real tough Chinaman and they offered Greer and Cameron seventy-five dollars to kill him.

Miss Hawkline sat naked on the floor of a room filled with musical instruments and kerosene lamps that were burning low. She was sitting next to a harpsichord. There was an unusual light on the keys of the harpsichord and there was a shadow to that light.

Coyotes were howling outside.

The lamp-distorted shadows of musical instruments made exotic patterns on her body and there was a large wood fire burning in the fireplace. The fire seemed almost out of proportion but its size was needed because the house was very cold.

There was a knock at the door of the room.

Miss Hawkline turned her head.

"Yes?" she said.

"Dinner will be served in a few moments," came the voice of an old man through the door. The man did not attempt to come into the room. He stood outside the door.

"Thank you, Mr. Morgan," she replied.

Then there was the sound of huge footsteps walking down the hall away from the door and eventually disappearing behind the closing of another door.

The coyotes were close to the house. They sounded as if they were on the front porch.

"We give you seventy-five dollars. You kill," the head Chinaman said.

There were five or six other Chinaman sitting in the small dark booth with them. The place was filled with the smell of bad Chinese cooking.

When Greer and Cameron heard the price of seventy-five dollars they smiled in that relaxed way they had that usually changed things very rapidly.

"Two hundred dollars," the head Chinaman said, without changing the expression on his face. He was a smart Chinaman. That's why he was their leader.

"Two hundred and fifty dollars. Where's he at?" Greer said.

"Next door," the head Chinaman said.

Greer and Cameron went next door and killed him. They never did find out how tough the Chinaman was because they didn't give him a chance. That's the way they did their work. They didn't put any lace on their killings.

While they were taking care of the Chinaman, Miss Hawkline continued to wait for them, naked on the floor of a room filled with the shadows of musical instruments. Lamp-aided, the shadows played over her body in that huge house in Eastern Oregon.

There was also something else in that room. It was watching her and took pleasure in her naked body. She did not know that it was there. She also did not know that she was naked. If she had known that she was naked she would have been very shocked. She was a proper young lady except for the colorful language that she had picked up from her father.

Miss Hawkline was thinking about Greer and Cameron, though she had never met them or even heard about them, but she waited eternally for them to come as they were always destined to come, for she was part of their gothic future.

Greer and Cameron caught the train to Portland, Oregon, the next morning. It was a beautiful day. They were happy because they liked riding the train to Portland.

"How many times now?" Greer asked.

"8 times straight through and 6 times we got off," Cameron said.

# · Magic Child ·

They had been whoring for two days when the Indian girl found them. They always liked to whore for a week or so in Portland before they settled down to thinking about work.

The Indian girl found them in their favorite whorehouse. She had never seen them before or heard about them either but the moment she saw them, she knew they were the men Miss Hawkline wanted.

She had spent three months in Portland, looking for the right men. Her name was Magic Child. She thought that she was fifteen years old. She had gone into this whorehouse by accident. She was actually looking for a whorehouse on the next block.

"What do you want?" Greer said. There was a pretty blonde girl about fourteen years old, sitting on his lap. She didn't have any clothes on.

"Is that an Indian?" she said. "How did she get in here?"

"Shut up," Greer said.

Cameron was starting to fuck a little brunette girl. He stopped what he was doing and looked back over his shoulder at Magic Child.

He didn't know whether to go on and fuck the girl or find out what the Indian girl was about.

Magic Child stood there without saying anything.

The little whore said, "Stick it in."

"Wait a minute," Cameron said. He started to shift out of the love position. He had made up his mind.

The Indian girl reached into her pocket and took out a photograph. It was the photograph of a very beautiful young woman. She wasn't wearing any clothes in the photograph. She was sitting on the floor in a room filled with musical instruments.

Magic Child showed the photograph to Greer.

"What's this?" Greer said.

Magic Child walked over and showed the photograph to Cameron.

"Interesting," Cameron said.

The two little whores didn't know what was happening. They had never seen anything like this before and they had seen a lot of things. The brunette suddenly covered up her vagina because she was embarrassed.

The blonde stared silently on with disbelieving blue eyes. Whenever a man told her to shut up, she always shut up. She had been a farm girl before she went into whoring.

Then Magic Child reached into the pocket of her Indian

dress and took out five thousand dollars in hundred dollar bills. She took the money out as if she'd been doing it all her life.

She gave Greer twenty-five of them and then she walked over and gave Cameron twenty-five of them. After she gave them the money, she stood there looking silently at them. She still hadn't said a word since she'd come into the room.

Greer sat there with the blonde whore still on his lap. He looked at the Indian girl and nodded OK very slowly. Cameron had a half-smile on his face, lying beside the brunette who was covering up her vagina with her hand.

# · Indian ·

Greer and Cameron left Portland the next morning on the train up the Columbia River, travelling toward Central County in Eastern Oregon.

They enjoyed their seats because they liked to travel on trains.

The Indian girl travelled with them. They spent a great deal of time looking at her because she was very pretty.

She was tall and slender and had long straight black hair. Her features were delicately voluptuous. They were both interested in her mouth.

She sat there exquisitely, looking at the Columbia River as the train travelled up the river toward Eastern Oregon. She saw things that interested her.

Greer and Cameron started talking with Magic Child after they were three or four hours out of Portland. They were curious as to what it was all about.

The girl hadn't said more than a hundred words since she had walked into the whorehouse and started to change their lives. None of the words were about what they were supposed to do except go to Central County and meet a Miss Hawkline who would then tell them what she would pay them five thousand dollars to do.

"Why are we going to Central County?" Greer said.

"You kill people, don't you?" Magic Child said. Her voice was gentle and precise. They were surprised by the sound of her voice. They didn't expect it to sound that way when she said that.

"Sometimes," Greer said.

"They got a lot of sheep trouble over that way," Cameron said. "I heard there was some killings there. 4 men killed last week and 9 during the month. I know 3 Portland gunmen who went up there a few days ago. Good men, too."

"Real good," Greer said. "Probably the best three men going I know of except for maybe two more. Take a lot to put those boys away. They went up there to work for the cattlemen. Which side is your bosslady on or does she want some personal work done?"

"Miss Hawkline will tell you what she wants done," Magic Child said.

"Can't even get a hint out of you, huh?" Greer said, smiling.

Magic Child looked out the window at the Columbia River. There was a small boat on the river. Two people were sitting in the boat. She couldn't tell what they were doing. One of the people was holding an umbrella, though it wasn't raining and the sun wasn't shining either.

Greer and Cameron gave up trying to find out what they were supposed to do but they were curious about Magic Child. They had been surprised by her voice because she didn't sound like an Indian. She sounded like an Eastern woman who'd had a lot of booklearning.

They'd also taken a closer look at her and had seen that she wasn't an Indian.

They didn't say anything about it. They had the money and that's what counted for them. They figured if she wanted to be an Indian that was her business.

# · Gompville ·

The train only went as far as Gompville, which was the county seat of Morning County and fifty miles away by stage-coach to Billy. It was a cold clear dawn with half-a-dozen sleepy dogs standing there barking at the train engine.

"Gompville," Cameron said.

Gompville was the headquarters of the Morning County Sheepshooters Association that had a president, a vice-president, a secretary, a sergeant at arms and bylaws that said it was all right to shoot sheep.

The people who owned the sheep didn't particularly care for that, so both sides had brought in gunmen from

Portland and the attitude toward killings had become very casual in those parts.

"We're running it tight," Greer said to Magic Child as they walked over to the stagecoach line. The stage to Billy left in just a few moments.

Cameron was carrying a long narrow trunk over his shoulder. The trunk contained a sawed-off twelve-gauge pump shotgun, a 25:35 Winchester rifle, a 30:40 Krag, two .38 caliber revolvers and an automatic .38 caliber pistol that Cameron had bought from a soldier in Hawaii who was just back from the Philippines where he had been fighting the rebels for two years.

"What kind of pistol is that?" Cameron had asked the soldier. They had been in a bar having some drinks in Honolulu.

"This gun is for killing Filipino motherfuckers," the soldier had said. "It kills one of those bastards so dead that you need two graves to bury him in."

After a bottle of whiskey and a lot of talk about women, Cameron had bought the gun from the soldier who was very glad to be on his way home to America and not have to use that gun any more.

# · Central County Ways ·

Central County was a big rangy county with mountains to the north and mountains to the south and a vast loneliness in between. The mountains were filled with trees and creeks.

The loneliness was called the Dead Hills.

They were thirty miles wide. There were thousands of hills out there: yellow and barren in the summer with lots of juniper brush in the draws and a few pine trees here and there, acting as if they had wandered away like stray sheep from the mountains and out into the Dead Hills and had gotten lost and had never been able to find their way back.

. . . poor trees . . .

The population of Central County was around eleven

hundred people: give or take a death here and a birth there or a few strangers deciding to make a new life or old-time residents to move away and never to return or come back soon because they were homesick.

Just like a short history of man, there were two towns in the county.

One of the towns was close to the northern range of mountains. That town was called Brooks. The other town was close to the southern range of mountains. It was called Billy.

The towns were named for Billy and Brooks Paterson: two brothers who had pioneered the county forty years before and had killed each other in a gunfight one September afternoon over the ownership of five chickens.

That fatal chicken argument occurred in 1881 but there was still a lot of strong feeling in the county in 1902 over who those chickens belonged to and who was to fault for the gunfight that killed both brothers and left two widows and nine fatherless children.

Brooks was the county seat but the people who lived in Billy always said, "Fuck Brooks."

# · In the Early Winds
# of Morning ·

Just outside of Gompville a man was hanging from the bridge across the river. There was a look of disbelief on his face as if he still couldn't believe that he was dead. He just refused to believe that he was dead. He wouldn't believe he was dead until they buried him. His body swayed gently in the early winds of morning.

There was a barbed-wire drummer riding in the stagecoach with Greer and Cameron and Magic Child. The drummer looked like a fifty-year-old child with long skinny fingers and cold-white nails. He was going to Billy, then onto Brooks to sell barbed wire.

Business was good.

"There's a lot of that going on around here now," he said, pointing at the body. "It's those gunmen from Portland. It's their work."

He was the only one talking. Nobody else had anything to say out loud. Greer and Cameron said what they had to say inside their minds.

Magic Child looked so calm you would have thought that she had been raised in a land where bodies hung everywhere like flowers.

The stagecoach drove across the bridge without stopping. It sounded like a minor thunderstorm on the bridge. The wind turned the body, so that it was watching the stagecoach drive up the road along the river and then disappear into a turn of dusty green trees.

# · "Coffee" with the Widow ·

A couple of hours later, the stagecoach stopped at Widow Jane's house. The driver always liked to have a cup of "coffee" with the widow on his way to Billy.

What he meant by a cup of coffee wasn't really a cup of coffee. He had a romance going with the widow and he'd stop the stagecoach at her house and just parade all the passengers in. The widow would give everybody a cup of coffee and there was always a big platter of homemade doughnuts on the kitchen table.

Widow Jane was a very thin but jolly woman in her early fifties.

Then the driver, carrying a ceremonial cup of coffee in

his hand, and the widow would go upstairs. All the passengers would sit downstairs in the kitchen, drinking coffee and eating doughnuts while the driver would be upstairs with the widow in her bedroom having his "coffee."

The squeaking of the bedsprings shook the house like mechanical rain.

# · Cora ·

Cameron had brought the trunk full of guns into the house with him. He didn't want to leave the guns unattended in the stagecoach. Greer and Cameron never carried guns on their persons not unless they intended to kill somebody. Then they carried guns. The rest of the time the guns stayed in the trunk.

The barbed-wire drummer sat there in the kitchen with a cup of coffee in his hand and from time to time he would look down at the trunk that was beside Cameron, but he never said anything about it.

He was curious enough, though, about Magic Child to ask her what her name was.

"Magic Child," Magic Child said.

"That's a pretty name," he said. "And if you don't mind me saying so, you're quite a pretty girl."

"Thank you."

Then, to be polite, he asked Greer what his name was.

"Greer," Greer said.

"That's an interesting name," he said.

Then he asked Cameron what his name was.

"Cameron," Cameron said.

"Everybody here's got an interesting name," he said. "My name is Marvin Cora Jones. You don't come across many men who's middle name is Cora. Anyway, I haven't and I've been to a lot of places, including England."

"Cora is a different kind of middle name for a man," Cameron said.

Magic Child got up and went over to the stove and got some more coffee for Greer and Cameron. She also poured some for the barbed-wire drummer. She was smiling. There was a huge platter of doughnuts on the table and everybody was eating them. Widow Jane was a good cook.

Like a mirror the house continued to reflect the motion of the bed upstairs.

Greer and Cameron each had a glass of milk, too, from a beautiful porcelain pitcher on the table. They liked a glass of milk now and then. They also liked the smile on Magic Child's face. It had been the first time that Magic Child had smiled.

"They named me Cora for my great-grandmother. I don't mind. She met George Washington at a party. She said that he was really a nice man but he was a little shorter than what she had expected," the barbed-wire drummer said. "I meet a lot of interesting people by telling them that my middle name is Cora. It's something that gets people's curiosity up. It's kind of funny, too. I don't mind people laughing because it is sort of funny for a man to have the name of Cora."

# · Against the Dust ·

The driver and the widow came down the stairs with their arms in sweet affection around each other. "It certainly was nice of you to show that to me," the driver said.

The widow's face was twinkling like a star.

The driver acted mischievously solemn but you could tell that he was just playing around.

"It's good to stop and have some coffee," the driver said to everybody sitting at the table. "It makes travelling a little easier and those doughnuts are a lot better than having a mule kick you in the head."

There was no argument there.

# · Thoughts of July 12, 1902 ·

About noon the stagecoach was rattling through the mountains. It was hot and boring. Cora, the barbed-wire drummer, had dozed off. He looked like a sleeping fence.

Greer was staring at the graceful billowing of Magic Child's breasts against her long and simple dress. Cameron was thinking about the man who had been hanging from the bridge. He was thinking that he had once gotten drunk with him in Billings, Montana, at the turn of the century.

Cameron wasn't totally certain but the man hanging from the bridge looked an awful lot like the guy he had gotten drunk with in Billings. If he wasn't that man, he was his twin brother.

Magic Child was watching Greer stare at her breasts. She was imagining Greer touching them with his casually powerful-looking hands. She was excited and pleased inside of herself, knowing that she would be fucking Greer before the day was gone.

While Cameron was thinking about the dead man on the bridge, *perhaps it was Denver where they had gotten drunk together,* Magic Child was thinking about fucking him, too.

# · Binoculars ·

Suddenly the stagecoach stopped on top of a ridge that had a meadow curving down from it. There was an Old Testament quantity of vultures circling and landing and rising again in the meadow. They were like flesh angels summoned to worship at a large spread-out temple of many small white formerly-living things.

"Sheep!" the driver yelled. "Thousands of them!"

He was looking down on the meadow through a pair of binoculars. The driver had once been an officer, a second lieutenant in the cavalry during the Indian Wars, so he carried a pair of binoculars with him when he was driving the stagecoach.

He had gotten out of the cavalry because he didn't like to kill Indians.

"The Morning County Sheepshooters Association has been working out this way," he said.

Everybody in the stagecoach looked out the windows and then got out as the driver climbed down from his seat. They stretched and tried to unwind the coils of travel while they watched the vultures eating sheep down below in the meadow.

Fortunately, the wind was blowing in an opposite manner so as not to bring them the smell of death. They could watch death while not having to be intimate with it.

"Those sheepshooters really know how to shoot sheep," the driver said.

"All you need is a gun," Cameron said.

# · Billy ·

They crossed the Shadow Creek bridge at suppertime. *There's nobody hanging from this bridge:* Cameron thought as the stagecoach drove into Billy.

There was an expression of pleasure on Magic Child's face. She was happy to be home. She had been gone for months, doing what Miss Hawkline had sent her to do, and they sat beside her. She looked forward to seeing Miss Hawkline. They would have many things to talk about. She would tell Miss Hawkline about Portland.

Magic Child's breathing had noticeably changed in sexual anticipation for the bodies of Greer and Cameron. They of course didn't know that Magic Child would soon be fucking them.

They could see that her breathing had changed but they

didn't know what it meant. They thought she was happy to be home or something.

Billy was noisy because it was suppertime. The smell of meat and potatoes was heavy on the wind. All the doors and windows in Billy were open. It had been a very hot day and you could hear people eating and talking.

Billy was about sixty or seventy houses, buildings and shacks built on both sides of a creek that flowed through a canyon whose slopes were covered with juniper brush that gave a sweet fresh smell to things.

Billy had three bars, a cafe, a big mercantile store, a blacksmith, and a church. It didn't have a hotel, a bank or a doctor.

There was a town marshal but there wasn't a jail. He didn't need one. His name was Jack Williams and he could be a mean motherfucker. He thought putting somebody in jail was a waste of time. If you caused any trouble in Billy, he'd punch you in the mouth and throw you in the creek. The rest of the time he ran a very friendly saloon, The Jack Williams House, and would buy a drink every morning for the town drunk.

There was a graveyard behind the church and the minister, a Fredrick Calms, was always trying to raise enough money to put a fence around the graveyard because the deer got in there and ate the flowers and stuff off the graves.

For some strange reason, it made the minister mad whenever he saw some deer among the graves and he'd start cursing up a storm, but nobody ever took putting a fence up around the graveyard very seriously.

The people just didn't give a shit.

"So a few deer get in there. That's no big thing. The minister is kind of crazy, anyway," was their general reaction to putting a fence around the graveyard in Billy.

# · The Governor of Oregon ·

Greer, Cameron and Magic Child went over to the black-smith's shop to get some horses for the ride out to Miss Hawkline's in the morning. They wanted to make sure the horses would be ready when they left at dawn.

The blacksmith had a collection of strange horses that he would rent out sometimes if he knew you or liked your looks. He'd had a bucket of beer along with his dinner that evening, so he was very friendly.

"Magic Child," he said. "Ain't seen you around for a while. You been someplace? Hear they're killing people over Gompville way. My name is Pills," holding out his beer-friendly hand to Greer and Cameron. "I take care of the horses around here."

"We need some horses in the morning," Magic Child said. "We're going out to Miss Hawkline's."

"I think I can do you up with some horses. Maybe one of them will get that far: if you're lucky."

Pills liked to joke about his horses. He was famous in those parts for having the worst bunch of horses ever assembled in a corral.

He had a horse that was so swaybacked that it looked like an October quarter moon. He called that horse Cairo. "This is an Egyptian horse," he used to tell people.

He had another horse that didn't have any ears. A drunken cowboy had bitten them off for a fifty-cent bet.

"I bet you fifty cents I'm so drunk I'd bite a horse's ears off!"

"God-damn, I don't think you're that drunk!"

And he had another horse that actually drank whiskey. They'd put a quart of whiskey in his bucket and he'd drink it all down and then he'd fall over on his side and everybody would laugh.

But the prize of his collection was a horse that had a wooden foot. The horse was born without a right rear foot, so somebody had carved him a wooden one, but the person had gotten confused in his carving, he wasn't really right in the head, anyway, and the wooden foot looked more like a duck's foot than a horse's foot. It really looked strange to see that horse walking around with a wooden duck foot.

A politician once came all the way from La Grande to look at those horses. It was even rumored that the governor of Oregon had heard about them.

# · Jack Williams ·

On their way over to Ma Smith's Cafe to have some dinner, Jack Williams, the town marshal, strolled out of his saloon. He was going someplace else but when he saw Magic Child, whom he liked a lot, and two strange men with her, he walked over to Magic Child and her friends to say hello and find out what was happening.

"Magic Child! God-damn!" he said and threw his arms around her and gave her a big hug.

He could tell that the two men did not work for a living and in appearance there was nothing about them that one would ever remember. They both looked about the same except they had different features and different builds. It was the way they handled themselves that was memorable.

One of them was taller than the other one but once you turned your back on them you wouldn't be able to remember which one it was.

Jack Williams had seen men similar to these before. Instinctively, without even bothering with an intellectual process, he knew that these men could mean trouble. One of them was carrying a long narrow trunk on his shoulder. He carried the trunk easily as if it were part of his shoulder.

Jack Williams was a big man: over six feet tall and weighed in excess of two hundred pounds. His toughness was legendary in that part of Eastern Oregon. Men with evil thoughts on their minds generally stayed clear of Billy.

Jack Williams wore a shoulder holster with a big shiny .38 in it. He didn't like to wear a regular gun belt around his waist. He always joked that he didn't like to have all that iron hanging so close to his cock.

He was forty-one years old and in the prime of health.

"Magic Child! God-damn!" he said and threw his arms around her and gave her a big hug.

"Jack," she said. "You big man!"

"I've missed you, Magic Child," he said. He and Magic Child had fucked a few times and he had a tremendous respect for her quick lean body.

He liked her a lot but sometimes he was a little awestruck and disturbed by how much she looked like Miss Hawkline. They looked so much alike that they could have been twins. Everybody in town noticed it but there was nothing they could do about it, so they just let it be.

"These are my friends," she said, making the introductions. "I want you to meet them. This is Greer and this is

Cameron. I want you to meet Jack Williams. He's the town marshal."

Greer and Cameron were smiling softly at the intensity of Magic Child's and Jack Williams' greeting.

"Howdy," Jack Williams said, shaking their hands. "What are you boys up to?"

"Come on now," Magic Child said. "These are my friends."

"I'm sorry," Jack Williams said, laughing. "I'm sorry, boys. I own a saloon here. Any time you want there's a drink waiting over there for you and it's on me."

He was a fair man and people respected him for it.

Greer and Cameron liked him immediately.

They liked people who had strong character. They didn't like to kill people like Jack Williams. Sometimes it made them feel bad afterwards and Greer would always say, "I liked him," and Cameron would always answer, "Yeah, he was a good man," and they wouldn't say anything more about it after that.

Just then some gunshots rang out in the hills above Billy. Jack Williams paid no attention to the shots.

"5, 6," Cameron said.

"What's that?" Jack Williams said.

"He was counting the gunshots," Greer said.

"Oh, that. Oh, yeah," Jack Williams said. "They're up there probably killing themselves or killing off their animals. Frankly, I don't give a fuck. Excuse me, Magic Child, I'm sorry. I've got a tongue that was hatched on an outhouse seat. I'm saving it for my old age. Instead of whittling, I'll stop cussing."

"What's the shooting about?" Greer said, nodding his head up toward the twilight hills towering above Billy.

"Oh, come on now," Jack Williams said. "You boys know better than that."

Greer and Cameron smiled softly again.

"I don't care what those cattle and sheep people do to each other. They can kill everyone of themselves off if they're going to be that stupid, just as long as they don't do it in the streets of Billy."

"That county sheriff from Brooks. Up there's his problem. I don't think he ever gets off his ass, not unless he's looking for a piece of ass. Oh, God, I've done it again. Magic Child, when will this tongue of mine ever learn?"

Magic Child smiled up at Jack Williams. "I'm glad to be back." She touched his hand gently.

That pleased the town marshal of Billy whose name was Jack Williams and who was known far and wide as a tough but fair man.

"I guess I'd better get along now," he said. "Glad you're back, Magic Child." Then he turned to Greer and Cameron and said, "Hope you boys from Portland have a good time here but just remember," he said, pointing at the hills. "Up there, not down here."

# · Ma Smith's Cafe ·

They had some fried potatoes and steaks for dinner and biscuits all covered with gravy at Ma Smith's Cafe, and the
people eating there wondered why they were in town, and
they had some blackberry pie for dessert, and the people,
mostly cowboys, wondered what was in the long narrow
trunk beside their table, and Magic Child had a glass of milk
along with her pie, and the cowboys were made a little
nervous by Greer and Cameron, though they didn't know
exactly why, but the cowboys all thought that Magic Child
sure was pretty and they'd sure like to fuck her and they
wondered where she had been these last months. They
hadn't seen her in town. She must have been someplace else

but they didn't know where. Greer and Cameron continued to make them nervous but they still didn't know why. One thing they did know, though, Greer and Cameron did not look like the kind of people who had come to Billy to settle down.

Greer thought about having another piece of pie but he didn't. It was a nice thought. He really liked the pie and the thought was as good as having another piece of pie. The pie was that tasty.

They heard half-a-dozen more gunshots back off in the hills while they were finishing their coffee. All the shots were methodical, aimed and well-placed. It was the same gun firing and it sounded like a 30:30. Whoever was firing that gun really thought about it every time they pulled the trigger.

# · And Ma Smith ·

Ma Smith, a cantankerous old woman, looked up from a steak she was frying for a cowboy. She was a big woman with a very red face and shoes that were much too small for her feet. She considered herself big enough every place else without having to have big feet, so she stuffed her feet into shoes that were much too small for them, which caused her to be in considerable pain most of her walking hours and led her to having a very short temper.

Her clothes were very sweaty and stuck to her as she moved around the big wooden stove that she was cooking over on a night that was already hot enough by itself.

Cameron counted the gunshots in his mind.

*1* . . .

*2* . . .

*3* . . .

*4* . . .

*5* . . .

*6* . . .

Cameron waited to count the seventh shot, but then there was silence. The shooting was over.

Ma Smith was angrily fussing around with the steak on the stove. It looked like the last steak she was going to have to cook that night and she was very glad for that. She'd had enough for the day.

"I bet they're killing somebody out there," the cowboy said whose steak was being cooked. "I've been waiting for the killing to work its way down here. It's just a matter of time. That's all. Well, I don't care who kills who as long as they don't kill me."

"You won't get killed down here," an old miner said. "Jack Williams will make sure of that."

Ma Smith took the steak and put it on a big white platter and brought it over to the cowboy who didn't want to get killed.

"How does this look?" she said.

"Better put some more fire under it," the cowboy said.

"Next time you come in here I'll just cook you up a big plate of ashes," she said. "And sprinkle some God-damn cow hair on it."

# · Pills' Last Love ·

They slept that night in Pills' barn. Pills got them a big arm-load of blankets.

"I guess I won't be seeing you tomorrow morning," Pills said. "You'll be off at daybreak, huh?"

"Yes," Magic Child said.

"If you change your mind or you want some breakfast or coffee or anything, just wake me up or come in the house and fix it yourself. Everything's in the cupboard," Pills said.

He liked Magic Child.

"Thank you, Pills. You're a kind man. If we change our minds, we'll come in and rob your cupboard," Magic Child said.

"Good," Pills said. "I guess you'll work out the sleeping arrangements OK." That was his sense of humor after a few buckets of beer.

Magic Child had a reputation in town for being generous with her favors. Once she had even laid Pills which made him very happy because he was sixty-one years old and didn't think he'd ever do it again. His last lover had been a widow woman in 1894. She moved to Corvallis and that was the end of his love life.

Then one evening, out of the clear blue, Magic Child said to him, "When was the last time you fucked a woman?" There had been a long pause after that while Pills stared at Magic Child. He knew that he wasn't that drunk.

"Years."

"Do you think you can get it up?"

"I'd like to try."

Magic Child put her arms around the sixty-one-year-old bald-headed, paunchy, half-drunk keeper of strange horses and kissed him on the mouth.

"I think I can do it."

# · In the Barn ·

Greer carried a lantern and Cameron carried the blankets and Magic Child trailed after them into the barn. She was very excited by the hard lean curve of their asses.

"Where's the best place to sleep here?" Cameron said.

"Up in the loft," Magic Child said. "There's an old bed up there. Pills keeps it for travellers to sleep in. That bed is the only hotel in town." Her voice was dry and suddenly nervous. She could just barely keep her hands off them.

Greer noticed it. He looked over at her. Her eyes darted like excited jade into his eyes and then out of them and he smiled softly. She didn't smile at all.

They carefully climbed the ladder up to the loft. It smelled sweetly of hay and there was an old brass bed beside the hay. The bed looked very comfortable after two days of travel. It shined like a pot of gold at the end of the rainbow.

"Fuck me," Magic Child said.

"What?" Cameron said. He had been thinking about something else. He had been thinking about the six gunshots off in the hills during dinner.

"I want you both," Magic Child said and passion broke her voice like an Aphrodite twig.

Then she took her clothes off. Greer and Cameron stood there watching. Her body was slender and long with high firm breasts that had small nipples. And she had a good ass.

Greer blew the lantern out and she fucked Greer first.

Cameron sat on a dark bale of hay while Magic Child and Greer fucked. The brass bed sounded alive as it echoed the motion of their passion.

After while the bed stopped moving and everything was quiet except for the voice of Magic Child saying thank you, thank you, over and over again to Greer.

Cameron counted how many times she said thank you. She said thank you eleven times. He waited for her to say thank you a twelfth time but she didn't say it again.

Then Cameron took his turn with Magic Child. Greer didn't bother to get out of bed. He just lay there beside them while they fucked. Greer felt too good to move.

After another while the bed fell silent. There wasn't a sound for a couple of moments and then Magic Child said, "Cameron." She said it once. That's all she said it. Cameron waited for her to say his name again or to say something else but she didn't say his name again and she didn't say anything else.

She just lay there affectionately stroking his ass like a kitten.

# · The Drum ·

The slamming of screen doors and dogs barking and the rattling of breakfast pots and pans and roosters crowing and people coughing and grumbling and stirring about: getting ready to start their day beat like a drum in Billy.

It was a silver early-in-the-morning drum that would lead to the various events that would comprise July 13, 1902.

The town drunk was lying facedown in the middle of the Main Street of town. He was passed out and at peace with the summer dust. His eyes were closed. There was a smile on the side of his face. A big yellow dog was sniffing at his boots and a big black dog was sniffing at the yellow dog. They were happy dogs. Both of their tails were wagging.

A screen door slammed and a man shouted so loudly that the dogs stopped their sniffing and wagging, "Where in the hell is my God-damn hat!"

"On your head, you idiot!" was the female reply.

The dogs thought about this for a moment and then they started barking at the town drunk and woke him up.

# · Welcome to the Dead Hills ·

They woke up at dawn the next morning and rode out on three sad horses into the Dead Hills. Their name was perfect. They looked as if an undertaker had designed them from left-over funeral scraps. It was a three-hour ride to Miss Hawk-line's house. The road was very bleak, wandering like the handwriting of a dying person over the hills.

There were no houses, no barns, no fences, no signs that human life had ever made its way this far except for the road which was barely legible. The only comforting thing was the early morning sweet smell of juniper brush.

Cameron had the trunk full of guns strapped onto the back of his horse. He thought it remarkable that the animal could still move. He had to think back a ways to remember a horse that had been in such bad shape.

"Sure is stark," Greer said.

Cameron had been counting the hills as they rode along. He got to fifty-seven. Then he gave up. It was just too boring.

"57," he said.

Then he didn't say anything else. Actually, "57" had been the only thing that he'd said since they left Billy a few hours before.

Magic Child waited for Cameron to explain why he'd said "57" but he didn't. He didn't say anything more.

"Miss Hawkline lives out here," Greer said.

"Yes," Magic Child said. "She loves it."

# · Something Human ·

Finally they came across something human. It was a grave. The grave was right beside the road. It was simply a pile of bleak rocks covered with vulture shit. There was a wooden cross at one end of the rocks. The grave was so close to the road that you almost had to ride around it.

"Well, at last we've got some company," Greer said.

There were a bunch of bullet holes in the cross. The grave had been used for target practice.

"9," Cameron said.

"What was that?" Magic Child said.

"He said there are nine bullet holes in the cross," Greer said.

Magic Child looked over at Cameron. She looked at him about ten seconds longer than she should have looked at him.

"Don't mind Cameron," Greer said. "He just likes to count things. You'll get used to it."

# · The Coat ·

They rode farther and farther into the Dead Hills which disappeared behind them instantly to reappear again in front of them and everything was the same and everything was very still.

At one time Greer thought he saw something different but he was mistaken. What he saw was exactly the same as what he had been seeing. He thought that it was smaller but then he realized that it was exactly the same size as everything else.

He slowly shook his head.

"Where does Pills get these horses?" Cameron said to Magic Child.

"That's what everybody wants to know," Magic Child said.

After while Cameron felt like counting again but because everything was the same it was difficult to find anything to count, so Cameron counted the footsteps of his horse, carrying him deeper and deeper into the Dead Hills and Miss Hawkline standing on the front porch of a gigantic yellow house, shielding her eyes against the sun with her hand and staring out into the Dead Hills. She was wearing a heavy winter coat.

# · The Doctor ·

Magic Child was very glad to be home and she considered
these hills to be home. You couldn't tell, though, that she
was happy because she wore a constant expression on her
face that had nothing to do with happiness. It was an anxious, slightly abstract look. It had been on her face since
they had awakened in the barn.

Greer and Cameron had wanted another go at her but
she hadn't been interested. She had told them that it was very
important they get out to Miss Hawkline's place.

"911," Cameron said.

"What are you counting now?" Magic Child said, in a
voice that sounded very intelligent. She was smart, too. She

had graduated at the head of her class at Radcliffe and had attended the Sorbonne. Then she had studied to be a doctor at Johns Hopkins.

She was a member of a prominent New England family that dated back to the *Mayflower.* Her family had been one of the contributing lights that led to the flowering of New England society and culture.

Surgery was her specialty.

"Hoofsteps," Cameron said.

# · The Bridge ·

Suddenly a rattlesnake appeared, crawling rapidly across the road. The horses reacted to the snake: by whinnying and jumping about. Then the snake was gone. It took a few moments to calm the horses down.

After the horses had been returned to "normal" Greer said, "That was a big God-damn rattler. I don't know if I've ever seen one that big before. You ever see a rattler that big before, Cameron?"

"Not any bigger," Cameron said.

"That's what I thought," Greer said.

Magic Child was directing her attention to something else.

"What is it, Magic Child?" Greer said.

"We're almost home," she said, now breaking out into a big smile.

# · Hawkline Manor ·

The road turned slightly, then went up over the horizon of a dead hill and from the top of the hill you could see a huge three-story yellow house about a quarter of a mile away in the center of a small meadow that was the same color as the house except for close to the house where it was white like snow.

There were no fences or outbuildings or anything human or trees near the house. It just stood there alone in the center of the meadow with white stuff piled close in around it and more white stuff on the ground around it.

There wasn't even a barn. Two horses grazed a hundred yards or so from the house and there was a huge flock of red chickens the same distance away on the road that ended at the front porch of the house.

The road stopped like a dying man's signature on a last-minute will.

There was a gigantic mound of coal beside the house which was a classic Victorian with great gables and stained glass across the tops of the windows and turrets and balconies and red brick fireplaces and a huge porch all around the house. There were twenty-one rooms in the house, including ten bedrooms and five parlors.

Just a quick glance at the house and you knew that it did not belong out there in the Dead Hills surrounded by nothing. The house belonged in Saint Louis or San Francisco or Chicago or anyplace other than where it was now. Even Billy would have been a more understandable place for the house but out here there was no reason for it to exist, so the house looked like a fugitive from a dream.

Heavy black smoke was pouring out of three brick chimneys. The temperature was over ninety on the hill top. Greer and Cameron wondered why there were fires burning in the house.

They sat there on their horses for a few moments on the horizon, staring down at the house. Magic Child continued smiling. She was very happy.

"That's the strangest thing I've ever seen in my life," Greer said.

"Don't forget Hawaii," Cameron said.

*Book* 2

· Miss Hawkline ·

# · Miss Hawkline ·

As they rode slowly down the hill toward the house the front door opened and a woman stepped outside onto the porch. The woman was Miss Hawkline. She was wearing a heavy long white coat. The woman stood there watching them as they rode down closer and closer to the house.

It seemed peculiar to Greer and Cameron that she should be wearing a coat on a hot July morning.

She was tall and slender and had long black hair. The coat flowed like a waterfall down her body to end at a pair of pointed high-top shoes. The shoes were made of patent leather and sparkled like pieces of coal. They could easily have come from the huge mound of coal beside the house.

She just stood there on the porch watching them approach. She made no motion toward them. She didn't move. She just stood there watching them as they came down the hill.

She was not the only one watching them. They were also being observed from an upstairs window.

When they were a hundred yards away from the house, the air suddenly turned cold. The temperature dropped about forty degrees. The drop was as sudden as the motion of a knife.

It was like journeying from summer into winter by blinking your eyes. The two horses and the huge flock of red chickens stood there in the heat watching them as they rode into the cold a few feet away.

Magic Child slowly raised her arm and affectionately waved at the woman who returned the gesture with an equal amount of affection.

When they were about fifty yards away from the house, there was frost on the ground. The woman took a step forward. She had an incredibly beautiful face. Her features were clean and sharp like the ringing of a church bell on a full moon night.

When they were twenty-five yards away from the house, she moved to the top of the stairs which went down eight steps to the yellow grass which was frozen hard like strange silverware. The grass went right up to the stairs and almost up to the house. The only thing that stopped the grass from directly touching the house were drifts of snow that were piled against the house. If it hadn't been for the snow, the frozen yellow grass would have been a logical extension of the house or a rug too big to bring inside.

The grass had been frozen for centuries.

Then Magic Child started laughing. The woman started laughing, too, such a beautiful sound, the sound of them together laughing with white steam coming out of their mouths in the cold air.

Greer and Cameron were freezing.

The woman ran down the stairs to Magic Child who slipped like a grape peeling off her horse and into the arms of the woman. They stood there for a moment with their arms around each other: still laughing. They were the same height and had the same color hair and the same build and the same features and they were the same woman.

Magic Child and Miss Hawkline were twins.

They stood there with their arms around each other: laughing. They were two beautiful and unreal women.

"I found them," Magic Child said. "They're perfect," with snow piled up around the house on a hot July morning.

# · The Meeting ·

Greer and Cameron got down off their horses. Miss Hawk-line and Magic Child had exhausted their very affectionate greeting and now Miss Hawkline had turned toward them and was ready to meet them.

"This is Miss Hawkline," Magic Child said, standing there and looking exactly like Miss Hawkline except that she was wearing Indian clothes and Miss Hawkline was turned out in a very proper New England winter wardrobe.

"Greer, Miss Hawkline," Magic Child said.

"I'm glad to meet you, Miss Hawkline," Greer said. He was smiling softly.

"It pleases me that you're here," she said.

"And Cameron," Magic Child said.

"You please me also," Miss Hawkline said.

Cameron nodded.

Then Miss Hawkline walked over to them and held out her hand. They both shook hands with her. Her hand was long and delicate but the grasp was strong. The grasp was so strong that it surprised them. It was another surprise in a day full of surprises. Of course all that had transpired so far to surprise them was just a downpayment on the things that would happen before the day was out.

"1, 2," Cameron said, looking at Miss Hawkline and Magic Child.

"I'm sorry," Miss Hawkline said, waiting for Cameron to finish what he was saying. Cameron didn't say anything more.

"That means he's glad to meet you," Magic Child said, smiling at Greer.

# · The Ice Caves ·

"Let's go inside the house," Miss Hawkline said. "And I'll tell you why Magic Child has brought you here and what you have to do to earn your money. Have you had breakfast yet?"

"We left at dawn," Magic Child said.

"It sounds as if breakfast is in order," Miss Hawkline said.

Greer and Cameron had noticed that the closer you got to the house, the colder the air became. The house towered above them like a small wooden mountain covered with yellow snow.

Greer saw something in a second-story window. It

floated like a small mirror. Then it was gone. He thought that there was somebody else in the house.

"You've noticed the cold, haven't you?" Miss Hawkline said as she led the way up the stairs to the porch.

"Yes," Greer said.

"There are ice caves under this house," Miss Hawkline said. "That's why it's cold."

# · The Black Umbrellas ·

They went into the house. It was filled with beautiful Victorian furniture and very cold.

"This way to the kitchen," Miss Hawkline said. "I'll cook up some breakfast. You boys look as if you could use some ham and eggs."

"I'm going upstairs to change," Magic Child said. She vanished up a curved mahogany staircase into the upper reaches of the house. Greer and Cameron watched after her until she was gone. Then they followed Miss Hawkline into the kitchen. It was very pleasant trailing after her. She had taken her coat off and she was wearing a long white dress with a high lace collar.

She had exactly the same kind of body that Magic Child

had. Greer and Cameron could imagine her without any clothes on, looking exactly like Magic Child which was a very good way to look.

"I'll cook some breakfast and then tell you what we want done. It's a long trip here from Portland. I'm glad that you came. I think we'll all turn out to be friends."

The kitchen was immense. There was a large window and you could look out and see the snow and the frost on the ground. A hot fire was burning in the stove and it was warm and comfortable in the kitchen.

Greer and Cameron sat down in chairs at the table and Miss Hawkline poured them cups of strong black coffee from a huge pot on the stove.

Then she got a ham and sliced off some big pieces and got them cooking on the stove. Some biscuits were made very quickly and put into the oven to bake. Greer and Cameron couldn't remember anybody making biscuits that fast and getting them into the oven so quickly.

Miss Hawkline was very skillful with her kitchen as she was with all the things of her life. She didn't say much as she went about cooking breakfast. Once she asked them if they liked Portland and they said that they did.

Greer and Cameron watched her very carefully, thinking about her every move, wondering what was going to happen next, knowing that this was all the beginning of some pretty strange adventures.

They looked casual, relaxed, not in a hurry at all, as if what had happened so far and this strange house perched over some ice caves with frost on the ground in summer were every day occurrences with them.

Cameron had brought the trunk full of guns into the house with them. He had left the trunk in the front hall next to a large elephant foot full of black umbrellas.

# · The First Breakfast ·

Just about the time breakfast was ready, Magic Child came into the kitchen. She was wearing exactly the same clothes that Miss Hawkline was wearing. Her hair was also combed the same way and she wore patent leather shoes that shined like coal. You could not tell the difference between Magic Child and Miss Hawkline.

They were the same person.

"How do I look?" Magic Child said.

"Fine," Greer said.

"You sure are 1 pretty girl," Cameron said.

"I'm so glad you're back," Miss Hawkline said, suddenly stopping breakfast to rush over and throw her arms around Magic Child again.

Greer and Cameron sat there, staring at these two identical visions of beautiful womanhood.

Miss Hawkline went back to the few minutes that took care of cooking breakfast and putting the food on the table where soon they were all gathered eating the first of many meals that they would eat together.

*Book 3*

· The Hawkline Monster ·

# · The Death of
# Magic Child ·

"Is anybody else going to have breakfast with us?" Greer said as he prepared to take his first bite of food. He was thinking about the flash of light he had seen in an upstairs window. He thought that the light was caused by a person.

"No," Miss Hawkline said. "There's nobody else in the house except us."

Cameron stared at his fork. It lay beside a plate that had a delicate Chinese pattern on it. He looked over at Greer. Then he picked up his fork and started eating.

"What do you want done?" Greer said. He had just finished swallowing a big mouthful of carefully chewed ham. Greer was a slow eater. He liked to enjoy his food.

"5,000," Cameron said. He still had some food in his mouth, so his words sounded a little bit lumpy.

"You have to kill a monster that lives under the house in the ice caves." Miss Hawkline said, looking over at Cameron.

"A monster?" Greer said.

"Yes, a monster," Magic Child said. "The monster lives in the caves. We want him dead. There's a basement with a laboratory in it above the caves. An iron door separates the laboratory from the caves and there's another iron door that separates the laboratory from the house. They're thick doors but we're afraid someday he'll break the doors down and get upstairs into the house. We don't want the monster running around the house."

"I can see that," Greer said. "Nobody likes monsters running around their house." He was smiling softly.

"What kind of a monster is this?" Cameron said.

"We don't know," Miss Hawkline said.

"We've never seen him," Magic Child said.

Ever since they had arrived at the house, Magic Child's personality had been changing. She was rapidly becoming more and more like Miss Hawkline. Her voice had been changing and the expressions on her face had been changing. She was growing closer and closer toward Miss Hawkline's way of talking and moving and doing things.

"But we can hear him howling in the ice caves and banging on the iron door with what sounds like a tail," Magic Child said, in a very Miss Hawkline manner.

Magic Child was becoming Miss Hawkline right in front of Greer and Cameron's eyes. By the time breakfast was over they were not able to tell the difference between them. Only their places at the table could tell who was Magic Child and who was Miss Hawkline.

"It's a terrible sound and we're afraid," Magic Child said.

Greer was thinking that as soon as they both stood up and you took your eyes off them for a second, you would not be able to tell which one was Magic Child and who was Miss Hawkline. He suddenly realized that Magic Child was going to die shortly in that kitchen and a second Miss Hawkline would be born and then there would be two Miss Hawklines and you wouldn't be able to tell the difference between them.

Greer felt a little sad. He liked Magic Child.

A few moments later, while they were all talking about the monster, both of the women got up and started moving around the kitchen, cleaning up after breakfast.

Greer kept his eye on the one that was Magic Child. He didn't want to lose her.

"We've never killed a monster before," Cameron said. Greer took his eyes accidentally off the women to listen to Cameron. Then he realized in horror what he had done and turned instantly back to the women but it was too late. He couldn't tell the difference between them.

Magic Child was dead.

# · The Funeral of
# Magic Child ·

"Which one of you is Magic Child?" Greer said.

The Hawkline women stopped their after-breakfast-kitchen-clean-up and turned toward Greer.

"Magic Child is dead," one of the women said.

"Why?" Greer said. "She was a nice person. I liked her."

"I liked her, too," Cameron said. "But that's the way it goes." Cameron had the kind of mentality that could accept anything.

"You die when you've lived long enough," one of the Hawkline women said. "Magic Child lived as long as she was supposed to live. Don't feel sad. It was a painless and needed death."

They were both smiling gently at Greer and Cameron. You could not tell the difference between the women now. Everything about them was the same.

Greer sighed.

"What about another name to tell the difference between you?" Greer said.

"There is no difference between us. We're the same person," one of the women said.

"They're both Miss Hawkline," Cameron said, to make it final. "I like Miss Hawkline and now we've got 2 of them. Let's call them both Miss Hawkline. Who gives a fuck in the long run?"

"That sounds fine," Miss Hawkline said.

"Yes. Just call us Miss Hawkline," Miss Hawkline said.

"I'm glad that's taken care of," Cameron said. "You have 1 monster in the basement. Right? And he needs killing."

"Not in the basement," Miss Hawkline said. "In the ice caves."

"That's the basement," Cameron said. "Tell us some more about this God-damn creature. Then we'll go down and blow its fucking head off."

# · The Hawkline Monster ·

The two Miss Hawklines sat back down at the table with Greer and Cameron and started telling the story of the Hawkline Monster.

"Our father built this house," Miss Hawkline said.

"He was a scientist teaching at Harvard," the other Miss Hawkline said.

"What's Harvard?" Cameron said.

"It's a famous college in the East," Miss Hawkline said.

"We've never been in the East," Greer said.

"Yes, we've been there," Cameron said. "We've been to Hawaii."

"That's not East," Greer said.

"Don't Chinamen come from China which is in the East?" Cameron said.

"It's not the same," Greer said. "Saint Louis is in the East and Chicago. Places like that."

"You mean *that* East," Cameron said.

"Yeah," Greer said. "*That* East."

"The monster—" Miss Hawkline said, trying to get back to the original subject which was the monster that dwelled in the ice caves under their house.

"Yeah," Greer said. "How in the hell did we get to talking about Hawaii? I hate Hawaii."

"I mentioned it," Cameron said. "Because we were talking about the East. I hate Hawaii, too."

"Hawaii's a dumb thing to bring up in this conversation. These women have a problem," Greer said. "They paid us their money to take care of it and let's get on with it and I know you hate Hawaii because I was standing right beside you on the fucking place. I know you remember that because you remember every fucking thing."

"The monster—" the other Miss Hawkline said, trying again to get back to the original subject which was the monster that dwelled in the ice caves under their house.

"I think the problem is this," Cameron said, totally ignoring Miss Hawkline and the monster. "If Miss Hawkline had said, '*back* East,' then I would have known right away what East she was talking about. She said, '*in* the East,' so I thought about Hawaii where we just came from. See, it's all because she said, '*in* the East,' instead of '*back* East.' Every idiot knows that Chicago is *back* East."

This was a very strange conversation that Greer and Cameron were having. They'd never had a conversation like this before. They had never talked to each other this way before either.

Their conversations always ran along very normally except for the fact that Cameron counted the things that passed through their lives and Greer had gotten used to that. He had to because Cameron was his partner.

Greer broke the spell of their conversation by suddenly turning his energy away from Cameron which was a very hard thing to do, and saying to Miss Hawkline, "What about your father? How does he figure in with this monster you've got hanging around your basement?"

"It's not in the basement!" Miss Hawkline said, getting a little mad. "It's in the ice caves that are underneath the basement. We have no monster in our basement! We just have our laboratory there."

She had become infected by the just-finished conversation between Greer and Cameron about the East.

"Let's start all over again," the other Miss Hawkline said. "Our father built this house . . ."

# · Hawaii Revisited ·

"He was teaching chemistry at Harvard and he also had a huge laboratory at home that he used for private experiments," Miss Hawkline said. "Everything was going along fine until the afternoon that one of the experiments got out of the laboratory and ate our family dog in the back yard. The next door neighbors were having a wedding reception in their garden when this happened. It was at this time that he decided to move to some isolated part of the country where he could have more privacy for his work.

"He found this location and built this house out here about five years ago with a huge laboratory in the basement and he was working on a new experiment that he called The Chemicals. Everything was going along fine until—"

"Excuse me," Greer said. "What about the experiment that ate your dog?"

"I'm coming to that," Hiss Hawkline said.

"I'm sorry," Greer said. "I was just a little curious. Continue. Let's hear what happened, but I already think I know what happened. Tell me if I'm wrong: one of the experiments ate your father."

"No," Miss Hawkline said. "The experiment didn't exactly eat our father."

"What exactly did it do?" Greer said.

Cameron was very carefully listening to everything.

"We're getting off on the wrong track again," the other Miss Hawkline said. "I don't know what's happening. This is very easy to explain but suddenly it's so complicated. I mean, I can't believe how strange our conversation has turned."

"It is sort of weird, isn't it?" Greer said. "It's like we can't say what we mean."

"I just forgot what we were talking about," Miss Hawkline said. She turned to her sister. "Do you remember what we were talking about?"

"No, I don't," the other Miss Hawkline said. "Was it Hawaii?"

"We were talking about Hawaii a little while ago," Greer said. "But we were talking about something else. What was it?"

"Maybe it was Hawaii," Cameron said. "We were talking about Hawaii. Isn't it a little bit colder in here now?"

"It does seem colder, doesn't it?" Miss Hawkline said.

"Yes, it's definitely colder," the other Miss Hawkline said. "I'll put some more coal in the stove."

She got up and went over to the stove. She opened the

lid on top to find the stove filled with coal because she had put some fresh pieces in just before she had sat down with her sister to talk to Greer and Cameron about the monster.

"Now, we were talking about Hawaii, right?" the other Miss Hawkline said.

"That's right," Greer said.

"It's a miserable place," Cameron said.

"I think we'd better go into another room," Miss Hawkline said. "This fire isn't warm enough."

They left the kitchen and went into one of the front parlors. They didn't say anything as they walked down the long hall to the parlor.

As soon as they stepped into the parlor, Greer turned to Miss Hawkline and almost shouted, "We were talking about the fucking monster, not Hawaii!"

"That's right," she almost yelled back and then they stood there staring at each other for a moment before Miss Hawkline said, "Something happened to our minds in the kitchen."

"I think you'd better tell us all about that monster right now," Cameron said. He looked grim. He didn't like his mind fucked around with by anybody, including monsters.

# · The Chemicals ·

The parlor was exquisitely furnished in an expensive and tasteful manner. They were all sitting down in beautiful chairs facing each other except for Cameron who was sitting on a couch by himself.

There was a generous coal fire burning in the fireplace and the room was warm and cozy, far different from the kitchen and they all could remember what they were talking about.

"Where's your father?" Greer said.

"He disappeared into the ice caves," Miss Hawkline said. "He went down there looking for the monster. He didn't come back. We think the monster got him."

"How do we figure into this?" Greer said. "Why didn't you go for the marshal and have him come out here and take a look into this? He seems to be a good man and he has a lot of interest in one of you."

"There are too many things to explain and we're sure that our father is dead. That the monster killed him," Miss Hawkline said.

Cameron listened carefully from the couch. His gray eyes looked almost metallic.

"We were instructed to complete our father's experiment with The Chemicals," the other Miss Hawkline said. "He told us that if anything ever happened to him that we were to complete The Chemicals. It was his last important experiment and we are following his instructions."

"We cannot stand the idea of our father having wasted his life," Miss Hawkline said. "The Chemicals meant so much to him. We consider it our duty to complete what he started. That's why we didn't get the marshal. We don't want people knowing what we are doing out here. That's why we got you to help us. We cannot concentrate fully on The Chemicals until the monster is dead. It's distracting having that thing down there, trying to get out of the ice caves and into the house to kill us. So if you kill it for us, it will make everything a lot simpler."

"What happened there in the kitchen?" Cameron said. "Why were we talking so strangely to each other? Why did we forget what we were talking about? Has that ever happened here before?"

There was a slight pause while the two Miss Hawklines looked at each other. Then one of them said, "Yes. Things like that have been happening ever since our father added a few more things to The Chemicals and then passed electricity through The Chemicals. We've been trying to figure out a way to correct the balance of The Chemicals and complete the experiment. We've been following the notes that our father left behind."

"I like the way you say, 'behind,'" Greer said. "Behind meaning that some God-damn monster ate him in the basement."

"Not the basement, the ice caves!" Miss Hawkline said. "The laboratory is in the basement!"

Cameron looked at the two Miss Hawklines. Everybody stopped talking because they could see that Cameron was going to say something.

"You girls don't seem to have much grief about your father's disappearance," Cameron said, finally. "I mean, you're not exactly in mourning."

"Our father brought us up a special way. Mother died years ago," Miss Hawkline said. "Grief doesn't figure into it that much. We loved our father a great deal and that's why we are going to finish his experiment with The Chemicals."

She was a little mad about this time. She wanted to get onto the killing of the monster and away from superfluous conversations about things that she wasn't really that much interested in: like mortal grief.

"Tell us more about what happened in the kitchen," Cameron said.

"Things like that happen," the other Miss Hawkline said. "They're always strange occurrences and they seldom duplicate themselves. We never know what's going to happen next."

"Once we found green feathers in all of our shoes," Miss Hawkline said. "Another time we were sitting in a parlor upstairs talking about something when suddenly we were nude. Our clothes just disappeared off our bodies. We never saw them again."

"Yes," the other Miss Hawkline said. "That made me so fucking mad. I really liked that dress. I bought it in New York City and it was my favorite dress."

Greer and Cameron had never heard an elegant lady use the word fuck before. They would get used to it, though, because the Hawkline women swore a lot. It was something they had learned from their father who had always been very liberal with his language, to the point of being a legend at Harvard.

Anyway: on with the story . . .

"Has anything bad ever happened?" Cameron said.

"No, all the things that happen are like children's pranks except the child has supernatural powers."

"What does supernatural mean?" Cameron said.

The Miss Hawklines looked at each other. Cameron didn't like the way they looked at each other. All the fuck they had to do was to tell him what it meant. That was no big deal.

"It means out of the ordinary," Miss Hawkline said.

"That's good to know," Cameron said. He did not say it in a pleasant way.

"Are you ever afraid of what those chemicals might come up with next?" Greer said, taking over the conversation from Cameron and trying to put it on a more comfortable level.

The Miss Hawklines were relieved. They hadn't meant to hurt Cameron's feelings with the word supernatural. They knew it was a dumb thing that they had done, looking at each other, wishing they hadn't done it.

"They're never evil things," Miss Hawkline said. She

was going to say malicious, but she changed her mind. "Just very annoying sometimes like my favorite dress disappearing off my body."

"What are those chemicals supposed to do when they're finished?" Greer said. "And is this the same stuff that ate the dog?"

"We don't know what it's supposed to do," Miss Hawkline said. "Our father told us when The Chemicals were completed that the answer to the ultimate problem facing mankind would be solved."

"What's that?" Cameron said.

"He didn't tell us," Miss Hawkline said.

# · The Dog ·

"You didn't answer the question about the dog," Cameron said.

"No, it wasn't The Chemicals," Miss Hawkline said. "They haven't eaten anything. They're just mischievous."

"Then what ate the dog?" Cameron said. He really wanted to know what ate the dog.

"It was an earlier batch of some stuff that Daddy had mixed up," Miss Hawkline said.

"Did it have anything to do with The Chemicals?" Cameron said. He had just picked up the habit of calling Professor Hawkline's last experiment The Chemicals.

Miss Hawkline did not want to say what she was about

to say. Cameron was watching carefully the expression on her face just before she spoke. She looked like a guilty child about to speak.

"Yes, it was an earlier stage of The Chemicals that ate the dog but Daddy took the stuff and flushed it right down the toilet."

Miss Hawkline was blushing now and staring down at the floor.

# · Venice ·

Miss Hawkline got up from the chair she was sitting gravely in like a captured child and went over to the fireplace to poke the coal.

Everybody waited for her to finish and come back to the conversation about The Chemicals, the dog being eaten, etc., and what other topics that might be of interest on July 13, 1902.

While they waited Cameron counted the lamps in the room, 7, the chairs, 6, the pictures on the walls, 5. The pictures were of things that Cameron had never seen before. One of the pictures was of a street lined with buildings. The street was filled with water. There were boats on the water.

Cameron had never seen a street with boats on it instead of horses.

"What in the hell is that?" he said, pointing to the picture.

"Venice," Miss Hawkline said.

Having finished with the fireplace Miss Hawkline sat back down and the conversation was resumed. Actually, something they had talked about earlier was repeated and then they went onto something else.

# · Parrot ·

"If The Chemicals can change your thoughts around in your head and also steal the clothes right off your body, I think you've got something there that could be dangerous," Greer said.

"It's the monster we're worried about," Miss Hawkline said.

"Which one?" Greer said. "I think you might have two of them here. And the one behind the iron door down there in the ice caves might be the one that will give us the least trouble."

"Let's go down and kill that fucker right now," Cameron said. "Let's be done with it and then we can think about other things if you want to think about them. I'm bored with all this talking. It's getting us nowhere. I'll go get the guns and then let's go down there and do the killing. Do you know what it looks like or how big it is or what the fuck it is, anyway?"

"No, we've never seen it," Miss Hawkline said. "It just howls and pounds on the iron door that's between the ice caves and the laboratory. We've kept the door locked ever since our father disappeared."

"What does it sound like?" Cameron said.

"It sounds like the combination of water being poured into a glass," Miss Hawkline said. "A dog barking and the muttering of a drunk parrot. And very, very loud."

"I think we're going to need the shotgun for this one," Cameron said.

# · The Butler ·

Just then there was a knock at the front door. The knock echoed through the house and brought silence upon everybody in the parlor.

"What's that?" Greer said.

"It's somebody knocking at the door," Cameron said.

Miss Hawkline got up and started toward the parlor door that led into the front hall.

"It's the butler," the other Miss Hawkline said, remaining in her chair.

"The butler?" Greer said.

"Yes, the butler," the other Miss Hawkline said. "He's been up in Brooks getting some things we ordered from *back* East for The Chemicals."

They heard Miss Hawkline open the front door and then her voice and another voice talking.

"Hello, Mr. Morgan," she said. "Did you have a good trip?"

Her voice was very formal.

"Yes, madam. I got all the things that you requested."

The butler answered her with the voice of an old man.

"You look a little tired, Mr. Morgan. Why don't you go freshen yourself up and then go to the kitchen and have a cup of coffee. A cup of coffee will make you feel better."

"Thank you, madam. I could stand to get some of this dust off me and a cup of coffee would be most refreshing after my journey."

"How was Brooks?" Miss Hawkline said.

"Dusty and depressing as always," Mr. Morgan said.

"Was everything we ordered there?" Miss Hawkline said.

"Yes," Mr. Morgan said.

"Good," Miss Hawkline said. "Oh, before you go, Mr. Morgan. My sister is back from Portland and she brought some guests with her who will be staying here with us for a while."

She brought Mr. Morgan into the parlor.

He ducked his head when he stepped through the door and into the room.

Mr. Morgan was 7 feet, 2 inches tall and weighed over 300 pounds. He was sixty-eight years old and had white hair and a carefully trimmed white mustache. He was an old giant.

"Mr. Morgan, this is Mr. Greer and Mr. Cameron. They have come all the way from Portland and have graciously agreed to kill the monster in the ice caves."

"I'm pleased to meet you both," the old giant butler said.

Greer and Cameron told the giant they were glad to meet him, too. The Miss Hawklines stood there watching the meeting, looking quite beautiful.

"This is truly good news," Mr. Morgan said. "That thing down there is a regular nuisance, pounding on the door and making such terrible noises. Sometimes it's hard to get a good night's sleep around here. The demise of that beast would greatly help in making this house a bit more tolerable to live in."

Mr. Morgan had never really approved of Professor Hawkline's move from Boston to the Dead Hills of Eastern Oregon. He also did not like the site that the professor had chosen to build the house on.

He excused himself and left very slowly, because he was so old, ducking his head again to get through the door. They could hear him walking slowly down the hall to his room. The heavy sound of his footsteps was very tired.

"Mr. Morgan has been with our family for thirty-five years," Miss Hawkline said.

"His previous employment involved working with a circus," the other Miss Hawkline said.

# · Getting Ready to Go to Work ·

"Let's go kill the monster and be done with it," Cameron said. "I'll get the guns."

"As soon as you get the equipment that you need, we'll take you down there," Miss Hawkline said.

Cameron went out into the hall and got the long narrow trunk full of guns that was beside the elephant foot umbrella stand. He came back into the parlor and put the trunk down on a couch and opened it.

"We'll need the shotgun for certain," Cameron said. He took out the sawed-off twelve-gauge shotgun and a box full of shells. They were 00 buckshot. He loaded the gun and then he put a handful of shells in his coat pocket.

Greer reached into the trunk and took out a .38 revolver. He loaded the pistol and put it into his belt.

Cameron took out the .38 caliber automatic pistol that had previously been used to kill Filipino insurgents. He put a clip of bullets in the butt of the gun and then he snapped back and pushed forward the receiver sending a shell into the chamber. He put the gun on safety and slipped it into his belt.

"How big are those caves?" Greer said to the nearest Miss Hawkline.

"Some of them are big," she said.

Cameron put an extra clip of bullets for the automatic in his coat pocket.

"Let's take a rifle with us," Greer said, reaching down into the trunk for the Krag. "We've never tried to stop a monster before. He might give us some extra work, so let's be prepared for it."

He loaded the box magazine of the Krag with shells and then he pulled the bolt back and slammed a shell into the chamber with a very quick motion. It surprised the Hawkline women and then it pleased them, knowing that Greer and Cameron were very experienced at their work.

Greer put another shell into the magazine, replacing the one that had just gone like a-cat-catching-a-mouse into the chamber.

The Krag had a leather strap on it and Greer slung the rifle over his shoulder. Then he put a handful of shells in his pocket. He was ready to earn his living.

"One of us is going to have to carry a lantern," Cameron said. "So he's only going to have one hand free if something happens real quick with that monster. You carry the lantern and this Filipino bustin' gun and I'll do the shotgun."

He handed the automatic pistol and the extra clip of bullets to Greer while saying, "Give me that .38 there."

Greer gave him the .38.

"I can get this rifle working real quick if we need it," Greer said. "And if the son-of-a-bitch jumps us, we've got enough stuff here to turn it into sausage."

"Can we be of any help?" Miss Hawkline said.

"No, girls. You'd just be in our way," Cameron said. "This is our line of work. So you just keep out of the way and we'll kill your monster for you. Who knows? Maybe we'll eat it for supper tonight. It might be real tasty."

# · Journey to the Ice Caves ·

The Hawkline women guided them down the hall to a flight of stairs that led to the laboratory and the ice caves.

They were halfway down the hall when they heard a heavy slow shuffling sound. It was the butler. He emerged, head ducking through a door, into the hall.

"You're going to kill the monster," he said, in a very old voice. His mouth moved and his voice seemed to come out moments later.

He towered above them.

His hair was white like the frost on the grass outside the house.

"The monster ate my master," the giant butler said. "If

only I were younger, I'd kill that monster with my bare hands."

His hands were huge and knotted with arthritis. Probably in their day they could have killed a monster but now they were in repose like old gray uneatable hams.

"You're going to kill the monster," the giant butler repeated. He was very tired from his trip to Brooks to pick up new things for The Chemicals. He was getting too old to make a trip that long.

The giant butler's eyelids were drooping.

"Thank God," he said. The word God almost lost itself in his throat. It sounded like somebody sitting down in an old chair.

# · The Door ·

The door that led to the basement was a heavy iron door with two bolts on it. Miss Hawkline pulled the bolts back.

There was also a large padlock on the door. The lock was very impressive. It looked like a small bank. Miss Hawkline took a huge key out of her dress pocket. She put the key into the padlock and started to turn it when suddenly there was a huge crashing noise behind them.

They were all startled and turned around to see the giant butler spread out, over 7 feet and 300 pounds, on the floor. He looked like a stranded boat in the hall.

Miss Hawkline ran down the hall toward him. The other Miss Hawkline followed like a shadow in her footsteps. They crouched on their knees over the giant butler.

Greer and Cameron stood there looking down. They already knew he was dead while the two Miss Hawklines still searched for life in his body. When they discovered that he was dead, they both stood up. Their faces were suddenly very composed. There were no tears in their eyes though they loved Mr. Morgan like an uncle.

Greer was holding a lantern in his hand and he had a rifle slung over his shoulder and a large pistol stuck in his belt. Cameron was holding a sawed-off twelve-gauge shotgun in his hands. The giant butler lay dead on the floor. The two Miss Hawklines stood there silent, totally composed, looking unreally beautiful.

"What do we do now, young ladies?" Cameron said. "Kill the monster or bury the butler?"

# · Thanatopsis Exit ·

"Do you know what I really want to do?" Miss Hawkline said.

"What?" Cameron said.

"I'd like to get fucked."

Cameron looked down at the giant butler and then at Miss Hawkline.

"I'd like to get fucked, too," the other Miss Hawkline said to her sister. "That's what I've been thinking for the last hour. It would be very nice to get fucked."

Greer and Cameron stood there with their guns while the giant butler lay there alone and forgotten with his death.

Greer took a deep breath. What the hell? You might as well do one thing as another.

"First things first," Cameron said. "Let's move this body out of the hall. Where do you want it?"

"That's a good question," Miss Hawkline said. "We could put him in his room or we could lay him out in a front parlor. I don't want to bury him now because I want to get fucked. I really want to get fucked. What a time to have a dead butler on your hands."

She was almost a little mad that the giant butler had taken this particular time and place to die. He looked awesome lying there in the hall.

"Hell, this is too much to think about," the other Miss Hawkline said. "Let's just leave him here for a while and take care of getting fucked."

"Well, you don't have to worry about him going any place," Cameron said.

So they just left the giant old butler lying dead on the hall floor and went off to get fucked, taking along with them a 30:40 Krag, a sawed-off shotgun, a .38 and an automatic pistol.

# · Thanatopsis Exit #2 ·

Greer as he made love to Miss Hawkline kept thinking about Magic Child. Miss Hawkline had a body that was exactly the same in its appearance and delightful movement as Magic Child's.

They were making love in a beautiful bedroom upstairs. The room had many delicate feminine things that were unfamiliar to Greer. The only thing wrong with the room was the cold. It was very cold in the room because of the ice caves under the house.

Greer and Miss Hawkline made love under many blankets in an incredibly ornate brass bed. Their passion had not allowed time to be spent building a fire in the fireplace.

Greer kept wondering as they made love if this Miss Hawkline were Magic Child. At one moment he almost said the name Magic Child to see if she would respond, but then he decided not to because he knew that Magic Child was dead and it did not make any difference in which Miss Hawkline she was buried.

# · After Making Love
## Conversation ·

After they finished making love, Miss Hawkline lay gently cuddling up against him and then she said, "Don't you think that it's kind of strange for us to be up here making love while the butler is lying down there dead in the hall and we haven't done anything about it?"

"Yes, it is a little strange," Greer said.

"I wonder why we didn't do anything about his body. You know, my sister and I are really very fond of Mr. Morgan. I've been lying here for the last few minutes thinking about why we haven't done anything about him down there. It's not a very gracious thing to go off fucking while your family butler, whom you love like an uncle, is lying dead in the hall of your house. That has got to be a very peculiar way to react."

"You're right," Greer said. "It sure is."

# · Mirror Conversation ·

In a bedroom down the hall a similar conversation was taking place between Miss Hawkline and Cameron. They had just finished making some very enthusiastic love in which Cameron had not a single thought about this woman being Magic Child. He had really enjoyed their fucking together and had not allowed any intellectual process to cloud his pleasure. He used his mind for more important things: like counting.

"I guess we'll have to do something about your butler," Cameron said.

"That's right," Miss Hawkline said. "I completely forgot about him. He's lying dead in the hall. He fell over dead and we left him there to come up here and get some fucking in. It totally slipped my mind. Our butler is dead. He's down there dead. I wonder why we didn't do anything about his body."

"I asked you if you wanted to do anything about it down there but you girls wanted to come up here and get fucked, so we came up here and that's what we've done," Cameron said.

"What?" Miss Hawkline said.

"What do you mean what?" Cameron said.

Miss Hawkline lay very puzzled beside Cameron. There was a slight furrow between her eyes. She was in such a state of consternation that it was almost like slight shock.

"We suggested it?" she said, after a few moments of trying to figure out what events led them away from the body of their beloved dead giant butler and upstairs into the arms of love-making.

"We . . . suggested . . . it?" she repeated very slowly.

"Yes," Cameron said. "You insisted upon it. I thought it was a little strange myself, but what-the-hell, you're running this show. If you want to fuck instead of taking care of your dead butler, that's your business."

"This is very unusual," Miss Hawkline said.

"You're right there," Cameron said. "It ain't your ordinary run-of-the-mill thing to do. I mean, I've never fucked before with a butler lying spread-out dead in the hall downstairs."

"I just can't believe it," Miss Hawkline said. By now she had turned her head away from Cameron and was staring up at the ceiling.

"He's dead," Cameron said. "You've got 1 dead butler downstairs in the hall."

# · Won't You
# Come Home, Bill Bailey,
# Won't You Come Home ? ·

Meanwhile, down in the laboratory above the ice caves everything was very quiet except for the movement of a shadow. It was a shadow that just barely existed between forms. At times the shadow would almost become a form. The shadow would hover at the very edge of something definite and perhaps even recognizable but then the shadow would drift away into abstraction.

The laboratory was filled with strange equipment. Some of it was of Professor Hawkline's invention. There were many work tables and thousands of bottles of chemicals and a battery to make electricity out here in the Dead Hills where there was no such thing.

The laboratory was very cold. Actually, it was frozen because of its proximity to the ice caves underneath it.

There were some cast iron stoves around the laboratory which were used to thaw it out when the Hawkline sisters came down here to work, trying to unravel the mystery of The Chemicals.

Though there was no formal light in the room, there was still a slight portion of light coming from somewhere which for the moment wasn't actually a definite place. The light was coming from somewhere in the laboratory but it was not possible to tell where the light originated.

The light of course was needed to establish the shadow as it played like a child's spirit between object and abstraction.

Then the light became a definite place and the shadow was then related to the place where the light was coming from which was a large leaded-crystal jar filled with chemicals.

This jar of chemicals was the reality and mission of Professor Hawkline's lifework. The Chemicals were what he had placed his faith and energy in before he disappeared. It was now being completed by his two beautiful daughters who lay in bedrooms upstairs with two professional killers, and his daughters were wondering why they had gone off making love to these men while the freshly-dead body of their beloved giant butler lay ignored, unattended and not even covered up on the front hall floor.

The Chemicals that resided in the jar were a combination of hundreds of things from all over the world. Some of The Chemicals were ancient and very difficult to obtain. There were a few drops of something from an Egyptian pyramid dating from the year 3000 B.C.

There were distillates from the jungles of South America and drops of things from plants that grew near the snowline in the Himalayas.

Ancient China, Rome and Greece had contributed things, too, that had found their way into the jar. Witchcraft and modern science, the newest of discoveries, had also contributed to the contents of the jar. There was even something that was reputed to have come all the way from Atlantis.

It had taken a tremendous amount of energy and genius to establish harmony between the past and present in the jar. Only a man of Professor Hawkline's talent and dedication could have joined these chemicals together in friendship and made them good neighbors.

There of course had been the earlier mistake that had caused Professor Hawkline and his family to leave the East but that batch had been flushed down the toilet and the professor had started over again out here in the Dead Hills.

Everything had been fully under control with the ultimate results of his experiments with The Chemicals promising a brighter and more beautiful future for all mankind.

Then Professor Hawkline passed electricity from the battery through The Chemicals and began the mutation which led to an epidemic of mischievous pranks occurring in the laboratory and eventually getting upstairs and affecting the quality of life in the house.

It started off with the professor finding black umbrellas in unlikely places in the laboratory and green feathers scattered about and once there was a piece of pie suspended in the air and the professor took to thinking too long about things that were not important. Once he spent two hours thinking about an iceberg. He had never spent more than a few moments previously in all of his life thinking about icebergs.

This mischief led to the clothes vanishing off the bodies of the Hawkline women upstairs and other things too silly to recount.

Sometimes the professor would think about his childhood. He would do this for hours at a time and then afterwards not be able to remember what he had been thinking about.

Then one day a horrible monster started howling and banging on the iron door that separated the ice caves from the laboratory. The monster was so strong that it shook the door. The professor and his daughters didn't know what to do. They were afraid to open the door.

The next day one of the Hawkline sisters went down to the laboratory to bring the professor some lunch. When he was working hard he didn't like to come upstairs to eat.

Because of his immense dedication he continued working, trying to reestablish the balance of The Chemicals while the monster from time to time hollered and banged on the door with its tail.

His daughter found the door to the ice caves open and the professor gone. She went to the door and yelled down into the caves, "Daddy, are you in there? Come out!"

A horrible sound came from deep in the caves and started coming through the darkness of the caves toward the open door and Miss Hawkline.

The door was immediately locked and one of the sisters, dressed like and thinking she was an Indian, went to Portland to find men qualified to kill a monster but who also possessed discretion, for they wanted to undo the mistake their father had made without public attention and finish his experiment with The Chemicals in a way that he would have approved of for the benefit of all mankind.

But they did not know that the monster was an illusion created by a mutated light in The Chemicals, a light that had the power to work its will upon mind and matter and change the very nature of reality to fit its mischievous mind.

The light was dependent upon The Chemicals for sustenance as an unborn baby relies upon the umbilical cord for supper.

The light could leave The Chemicals for brief periods of time but it had to return to The Chemicals to revitalize itself and to sleep. The Chemicals were like a restaurant and a hotel for the light.

The light could translate itself into small changeable forms and it had a shadow companion. The shadow was a buffoon mutation totally subservient to the light and quite unhappy in its role and often liked to remember back to the days when harmony reigned in The Chemicals and Professor Hawkline was there, singing popular songs of the day:

"Won't you come home, Bill Bailey, won't you come
    home?
She moans de whole day long;
I'll do de cooking, darling, I'll pay de rent;
I knows I've done you wrong."

As he poured a drop of this and a drop of that into The Chemicals in hopes for a better world, little realizing that each drop led him closer and closer to the day when he would pass electricity through The Chemicals and suddenly evil mischief would be created and the harmony of The Chemicals would be lost forever and soon the mischief would be turned in all its diabolical possibilities upon himself and his lovely daughters.

A lot of the contents of The Chemicals were not happy with what had happened since the electricity had been passed through them and the mutation occurred that created evil.

One of the chemicals had managed to completely separate itself from the rest of the compound. The chemical was very unhappy with the recent turn of events and the disappearance of Professor Hawkline because it had wanted very much to help mankind and make people smile.

The chemical now cried a lot and kept to itself near the bottom of the jar.

There were of course chemicals who were basically evil in nature and glad to be free of the professor's good-neighbor policy who exulted now in the goofy terror the light, which was the Hawkline Monster, inflicted upon its hosts, the Hawklines, and anybody who came near them.

The light possessed unlimited possibilities and took a special pride in using them. Its shadow was disgusted with the whole business and trailed, dragging its feet reluctantly behind.

Whenever the Hawkline Monster left the laboratory, drifting up the stairs and then slipping like melted butter under the iron door that separated the laboratory from the house, the shadow always felt as if it were going to throw up.

If only the professor were around, if only that terrible fate had not befallen him, he would still be singing:

"Me and Mamie O'Rorke,
Tripped the light fantastic,
On the sidewalks of New York."

# · The Hawkline Orchestra ·

Greer and Cameron and the Hawkline women, who were still mystified by their behavior, returned clothes to their bodies and all joined together in a music room on the same floor as the bedrooms that they had just finished making love in.

Greer and Cameron put their guns down on the top of a piano. Miss Hawkline went downstairs and made some tea and brought it back up on a silver platter and they all sat in the music room surrounded by harpsichords, violins, cellos, pianos, drums, organs, etc. It was a very large music room.

To make tea Miss Hawkline had to step around the body of the giant butler in the hall downstairs.

Greer and Cameron had never had tea before but they decided to try it because what-the-hell with all the things that were going on in this huge yellow house that was so weird that it almost breathed, straddling some ice caves that penetrated like frozen teeth deep into the earth.

Greer and Cameron had wanted to do something with the dead body of the giant butler as soon as they were finished with the living bodies of the Hawkline women, but the women insisted that they all have tea first before getting onto the disposal of the butler who was still sprawled out like an island in the hall.

A freshly-started fire was burning in the music room fireplace.

"Do you like your tea?" Miss Hawkline said. She was sitting beside Greer on a couch next to a harp.

"It's different," Greer said.

"What do you think, Cameron?" the other Miss Hawkline said.

"It doesn't taste like coffee," Cameron said. He counted all the musical instruments in the room: *18.* Then he said to the closest Miss Hawkline, "You have enough musical stuff here to start a band."

"We've never thought about it in that way," the Miss Hawkline said.

# · The Butler Possibilities ·

"What are we going to do with the butler's body?" Cameron said.

"That is a problem," Miss Hawkline said. "We'll really miss him. He was like an uncle to us. Such a good man. Huge but gentle as a fly."

"Why don't we start by moving him out of the hall. It's hard walking around him," Cameron said.

"Yes, we should move him," the other Miss Hawkline said.

"Why didn't we do that before we sat down here and started drinking this stuff?" Cameron said, looking disdainfully at his cup of tea. It was very apparent that Cameron was not going to be converted to the geniality of tea drinking. It was, you might say, not his cup of tea.

"I think we should bury him," Miss Hawkline said, thinking for a few seconds.

"You have to get him out of the hall if you want to put him into the ground," Cameron said.

"Precisely," the other Miss Hawkline said.

"I think we'll need a coffin," Miss Hawkline said.

"2 coffins," Cameron said.

"Do you gentlemen know how to make a coffin?" the other Miss Hawkline said.

"Uh-uh," Greer said. "We don't make coffins. We fill them."

"I think it would draw too much attention to us if we were to go into town and have one of the townspeople make us one," Miss Hawkline said.

"Yes, we don't want anybody coming out here and investigating into our business," the other Miss Hawkline said.

"Definitely not," Miss Hawkline replied, taking a very lady-like sip of tea.

"Let's plant him outside," Greer said. "We'll just dig a hole, put him in it, cover him up and it'll all be taken care of."

"We don't want to bury him close to the house," Cameron said. "The ground's frozen hard around this place and I'll be fucked if I'm going to dig a hole that big in frozen ground."

"We'll dig a hole outside of the frozen ground and then drag him out of the hall and put him into the hole," Greer said.

"It's sad to think of our beloved butler Mr. Morgan

in these terms," Miss Hawkline said. "I knew he was getting along in years and that someday he would die because, as we all know, death is inevitable, but I had never thought about what a problem the hugeness of his body would make. It's just something you don't think about."

"You didn't think he was going to turn into a dwarf when he died, did you?" Cameron said.

# · On the Way to a Butler Possibility ·

As they started downstairs to take care of the butler which meant guiding him to his eternal resting place, a hole in the ground, they passed the open door of a room that had a pool table in it. It was a beautiful table with a crystal chandelier hanging above it.

The door had been closed when Greer and Cameron came upstairs to fuck the Hawkline women.

"Look, a pool table," Cameron said, carrying a shotgun. He stopped momentarily to admire the pool table. "Sure is 1 fine-looking table. Maybe we can play some pool after we bury the butler and kill the monster."

"Yeah, some pool would be nice after we finish our

work," Greer said, with a 30:40 Krag slung over his shoulder and an automatic pistol in his belt.

"That's a pretty lamp, too," Cameron said, looking at the chandelier.

The room was illuminated by sunlight coming in the windows. Light from the windows gathered in the chandelier which reflected delicate green flowers from the pool table.

But there was also another light in the flowery pieces of glass that hung like a complicated garden above the table. The light moved very subtly through the pieces of glass and it was followed by a trailing, bumbling child-like shadow.

Greer, for a second, thought he saw something moving in the chandelier. He looked up from the pool table to stare at the chandelier and sure enough there was a light moving across the pieces of crystal. The light was followed by an awkward dark motion.

He wondered what could cause the light to move in the chandelier. None of the pieces of crystal were moving. They were absolutely still.

"There's a light moving in the chandelier," he said, walking into the room to investigate. "It must be reflecting off something outside."

He went over to a window and looked out. He saw the frost around the house circling out for a hundred yards and then stopping as summer took over the grass and the Dead Hills beyond.

Greer could see nothing moving outside that could cause a light to reflect in the chandelier. He turned back around and the light was gone.

"It's gone now," he said. "That's funny. There was nothing outside to start it."

"Why all this attention to a reflection?" Miss Hawkline said. "We have a dead butler lying in the hall. Let's do something about that."

"Just curiosity," Greer said. "The only reason that I'm still alive is because I'm a very curious person. It pays to keep on your toes."

He looked again at the chandelier but the strange light was gone. He did not know that the light was hiding on the pool table, near a side pocket, and there was a shadow hiding there, too.

"That light seemed familiar," Greer said. "I've seen it someplace before."

The light and the shadow held their breath, waiting for Greer to leave the room.

# · A Surprise ·

As they descended the spiral staircase to the main floor of the house, Miss Hawkline said to her sister, "The funniest thing happened a little while ago."

"What was that?"

"It's really strange," she said.

"Well, what was it?"

Greer and Cameron were trailing behind the Hawkline sisters. They moved so gracefully that Greer and Cameron were almost spellbound. The sisters moved without making a sound on the stairs. They moved in the same manner as two birds gliding slowly on the wind.

Their voices delicately punctuated the air like the invisible movement of peacock fans.

"I found some Indian clothes hanging in my closet. I didn't put them there," Miss Hawkline said. "Do you have any idea where they came from?"

"No," her sister said. "I've never seen any Indian clothes around here."

"It's really strange," Miss Hawkline said. "They're our size."

"I wonder where they came from," the other Miss Hawkline said.

"A lot of very strange things have been happening around here," Miss Hawkline answered.

Greer and Cameron looked at each other and they had something more to think about.

# · The Butler Conclusion ·

When they finally arrived at the body of the dead butler, they really had a surprise waiting for them. One of the Hawkline women put her hand up to her mouth as if to stifle a scream. The other Miss Hawkline turned white as a ghost. Greer sighed. Cameron put his finger in his ear and scratched it. "What the fuck next?" he said.

Then they just stood there staring at the butler's body. They stared at it for a long time.

"Well," Greer said, finally. "It's going to make burying him a lot easier."

Lying on the floor in front of them was the body of the butler but it was only thirty-one inches long and weighed less than fifty pounds. The dead body of the giant butler had been changed into the body of a dwarf. It was almost lost in folds of giant clothes. The pant legs were barely occupied and the coat was like a tent wrapped around the corpse of the butler.

At the end of a huge pile of clothes, there was a small head sticking out of a shirt. The collar of the shirt surrounded the head like a hoop.

The expression, which was of quiet repose, gone to meet his Maker, as they say, on the butler's face had remained unaltered in his transformation from a giant into a dwarf but of course the expression was much smaller.

# · Mr. Morgan,
# Requiescat in Pace ·

It did make burying the butler simpler. While Greer dug a
small grave outside the house, just beyond the influence of
frost, Miss Hawkline went upstairs and got a suitcase.

# · Prints ·

After the funeral with appropriate words of bereavement over a very small grave and a little cross, everybody went back into the house and gathered in a front parlor.

Greer and Cameron no longer had their guns with them. They had put them away in the long narrow trunk which was back beside the elephant foot umbrella stand. They only carried a gun when they were going to use one. The rest of the time the guns stayed in the trunk.

Cameron put some coal on the fire.

The two Miss Hawklines were sitting next to each other on a love seat. Greer sat across from them in a huge easy chair with a bear's head carved on the end of each armrest.

Cameron stood beside the fire, after having helped it out, facing the room and the troubled eyes of his contemporaries. He looked over at a table that had some cut-crystal decanters of liquor and fine long-stemmed crystal glasses that were keeping company on a silver platter.

"I think we need something to drink," he said.

Miss Hawkline got up from the love seat and went over to the table and poured them all glasses of sherry which they were momentarily sipping.

She returned to the side of her sister on the love seat and everybody was exactly as they were before Cameron made the suggestion except they had glasses in their hands.

It had been a delicately choreographed event like making different prints of a photograph except that one of the prints had glasses of sherry in it.

# · Magic Child Revisited ·

"I'd like to ask you girls a question," Greer said, but first he took a sip from his glass of sherry. Everybody in the room watched him carefully take his sip. He held the liquor in his mouth for a moment before he swallowed it. "Have either of you ever heard of somebody called Magic Child?" he said.

"No," Miss Hawkline said.

"The name's not familiar," the other Miss Hawkline replied. "It's a funny name, though. Sounds like an Indian name."

They both looked puzzled.

"That's what I thought," Greer said, looking over at Cameron standing beside the fireplace. The coal burned silently and smoke journeyed upward in departure from this huge yellow house standing in a field of frost at the early part of this century.

Greer as he looked over at Cameron suddenly noticed that part of the fire was not burning and part of the smoke just beyond it was not moving upward but was just hovering above flames of a slightly different color that did not burn.

He thought about the strange reflection in the poolroom chandelier. The fire that did not burn resembled that reflection.

He looked away from Cameron and back to the Hawkline women sitting primly beside each other on the love seat. "Who is Magic Child and what does she have to do with us?" Miss Hawkline said.

"Nothing," Greer said.

# · Return to the Monster ·

"I guess we should think about killing the monster down there in the basement," Cameron said and the Hawkline women didn't say anything. "We've been here all day and we haven't gotten around to that yet. So many things have been happening. I'd like to get that God-damn monster out of the picture, so we can get onto something else because there sure as hell seems to be something else here to get onto. What do you think, Greer? Time for a little monster killing?"

Greer looked casually over at Cameron but at the same time his vision took in the fireplace. The fire that did not burn and the smoke that did not move were gone. It was a normal fire now. He looked back at the Hawkline women and casually but carefully around the room.

"Did you hear me?" Cameron said.

"Yeah, I heard you," Greer said.

"Well, what do you think? A little monster killing?"

The Hawkline sisters were both wearing identical pearl necklaces. The necklaces floated gracefully about their necks.

But some of the pearls were glowing more brightly than the other pearls and some locks of hair hanging long about their necks seemed slightly darker than the rest of their hair.

"Yes, we should get around to killing the monster," Greer said. "That's what we're here for."

"Yeah, I think that's what we should do," Cameron said. "And then find out what's causing all these crazy things to happen around here. I never saw a man buried in a suitcase before."

# · Questions Near Sunset ·

The house was by now casting long shadows out across the frost as the sun was nearing its departure from the Dead Hills and Eastern Oregon and all the rest of Western America while Greer was asking the Hawkline women some last minute questions.

"And you've never seen the monster?" Greer said to Miss Hawkline.

"No, we've just heard it screaming down in the caves and we've heard it banging on the iron door that locks the caves off from the laboratory. It's very strong and can shake the door. The door's thick, too. Iron."

"But you've never seen it?"

"No, we haven't."

"And the door's been locked ever since your father disappeared?"

"Yes," Miss Hawkline said.

The pearls about the Hawkline sisters' throats had grown a little more intense in light, almost approaching a diamond-like quality. Greer saw a motion in the darkness of their hair. It was as if their hair had moved but it hadn't moved. Something had shifted in their hair. Greer thought for a second. Then he realized that it was the color of their hair that had moved.

"And sometimes you hear screams?"

"Yes, we can hear them all over the house and we can hear the banging on the iron door, too," Miss Hawkline said.

"How often?"

"Every day or so," Miss Hawkline said.

"We haven't heard anything," Greer said.

"Sometimes it's like that," the other Miss Hawkline said. "Why all these questions? We've already told you everything that we know and now we're telling it to you again."

"Yeah," Cameron said. "I want to get that monster out of the God-damn way."

"OK," Greer said. "Let's kill the monster," while letting his vision casually brush past the necklaces about the Hawkline sisters' throats.

The necklaces were staring back.

# · What Counts ·

But now the sun was down and early twilight had sub-
stituted itself on the landscape and though everybody was
ready to kill the monster, they were also very hungry and
soon their hunger got the best of them and killing the monster was put off until after supper which the Hawkline
women returned to the kitchen to prepare while Greer
and Cameron stayed on in the parlor.

When the Hawkline sisters departed, the strange light
stayed on the pearls and the moving dark color remained
in their hair and they unknowingly transported them to the
kitchen which was fine with Greer because he wanted to
talk about them with Cameron.

Greer started to tell Cameron what he had seen but Cameron interrupted him by saying, "I know. I've been watching them. I saw them in the hall by the butler's body after it got changed into a dwarf person. They were on the shovel while you were digging the grave and I saw them when I was putting my clothes on after fucking one of those Hawkline women."

"Did you see them in the chandelier above the pool table?" Greer said.

"Oh, yeah. But I wish you hadn't been so obvious about going in there and looking for them. I don't want to make them nervous and know that we know about them."

"You saw them here in the room?" Greer said.

"Sure. In the fire. Why do you think I was standing over there? because I wanted a hot ass? I wanted a closer look. They're gone now with the Hawkline women, so what do you think? I know what I think. I don't think we have to go down in the ice caves to find that fucking monster. I think we only have to go as far as the basement and those fucking chemicals that their crazy father was working on."

Greer smiled at Cameron.

"Sometimes you surprise me," Greer said. "I didn't know that you were picking up on it."

"I count a lot of things that there's no need to count," Cameron said. "Just because that's the way I am. But I count all the things that need to be counted."

# · But Supper First,
# Then
# the Hawkline Monster ·

Greer and Cameron decided to have supper first before
they dealt with The Chemicals in the laboratory and search
out what they thought would lead them to the Hawkline
Monster.

"We'll just play like we're going down into the ice caves
and blast out whatever, but when we get down to the basement we'll come up with some excuse to linger around down
there and if we come across something interesting, maybe
like The Chemicals, we'll shoot it," Cameron said. "But
first let's enjoy a good supper and not let on at all that we
know about that light and its shadow sidekick."

"OK," Greer said. "You've got it all pegged."

Then the Hawkline sisters came into the room. They had changed their dresses. They were now wearing dresses with very low necklines that accentuated beautiful young breasts. They both had tiny waists and the dresses showed them to advantage.

"Supper's ready, you hungry monster killers!"

The Hawkline women smiled at Greer and Cameron. "You need energy if you're going to kill a monster."

Greer and Cameron smiled back.

The same necklaces were still about the Hawkline sisters' throats and the light and the shadow were still there. The light looked comfortable in the necklaces and the shadowy dark color that could move was at rest in their long flowing hair.

*At least the Hawkline Monster has good taste,* Greer thought.

# · Counting the Hawkline Monster ·

During supper Greer and Cameron casually watched the Hawkline Monster about the throats and in the hair of the Hawkline sisters.

The monster was very informal during the meal. Its light diminished in the necklaces and the shadowy moving color in the sisters' hair was motionless, fading almost into the natural color of their hair.

The meal was steaks and potatoes and biscuits and gravy. It was a typical Eastern Oregon meal and eaten with a lot of gusto by Greer and Cameron.

Greer sat there thinking about the monster and thinking about how this was still the same day they had awakened in a barn in Billy. He thought about all the events that had so far transpired.

It really had been a long day with the prospects of much more to follow: Events that would lead him and Cameron to attempt to deprive the Hawkline Monster of its existence and the strange powers that it possessed sitting across the table from them, staring out of two necklaces about the throats of two beautiful women who were completely un-suspecting, at faith with their jewelry.

Cameron counted random things in the room. He counted the things on the table: dishes, silverware, plates, etc. . . . *28, 29, 30,* etc.

It was something to do.

Then he counted the pearls that the Hawkline Monster was hiding in: . . . *5, 6,* etc.

# · The Hawkline Monster
in the Gravy ·

Toward the end of supper the Hawkline Monster left the necklaces and got onto the table. It condensed itself into the space of a serving spoon that was in a large bowl of gravy on the table. The shadow of the monster lay on top of the gravy pretending that it was gravy.

It was very difficult for the shadow to pretend that it was gravy but it worked hard at the performance and sort of pulled it off.

Cameron was amused by the monster getting on the table and he understood how difficult it was for the shadow to pretend that it was gravy.

"Sure is good gravy," Greer said to Cameron.

"Yeah," Cameron said, looking over at Greer.

"You boys want some more gravy?" Miss Hawkline said.

"It sure is good," Greer said. "What about you, Cameron, more gravy?"

The shadow of the Hawkline Monster was lying as flat as it could on top of the gravy. The monster itself was slightly uncomfortable in the spoon that had a little more reflection to it than it should have had.

"I don't know. I'm pretty full now. But . . ." Cameron put his hand on the spoon. He was now touching the Hawkline Monster. The spoon, though it was in a bowl of hot gravy, was cold.

Cameron casually thought about how in the fuck he could kill the monster but he couldn't think of a way to kill a spoon, so he just used the Hawkline Monster to put some more gravy on his potatoes.

The monster obliged and fulfilled the function of a spoon. The shadow squirmed off the spoon when Cameron lifted the gravy from the serving bowl and it fell very awkwardly back into the bowl.

The shadow was very uncomfortable, almost sweating.

Cameron put the spoon back in the bowl and again disturbed the shadow which was now on the edge of panic.

"How about you, Greer? You want some more of this good gravy?"

The Hawkline sisters were pleased that their gravy was getting such rave notices.

"No, Cameron. Good as it is, I'm just too full," Greer said. "I think I'll just sit here and watch you enjoy it. I like to watch a man eat who likes what he's eating."

The shadow thought that it was going to throw up.

# · Parlor Time Again ·

After supper they retired to a front parlor leaving the Hawkline Monster dangling spoon-like in some gravy. There
was a large painting of a nude woman on the parlor wall.

Greer and Cameron looked at the painting.

The Hawkline Monster did not follow them into the
parlor. It went downstairs to the laboratory to get some
rest in The Chemicals. It was tired. So was its shadow.
Supper had been very long for them.

"Our father was fond of naked women," Miss Hawkline
said.

Coffee was served in the parlor with snifters of cognac
by the Hawkline sisters who looked even prettier if that were
possible.

Greer and Cameron kept looking at the nude painting of the woman and then at the Hawkline sisters who knew what they were doing but acted as if they didn't. They could have chosen a different parlor. They were excited by the situation. The only way they showed their excitement, though, was by a slight increase in their breathing.

"That's 1 pretty painting," Cameron said.

The sisters did not answer him.

They smiled instead.

Greer and Cameron while paying attention to the nude painting and the beauty of the Hawkline women had carefully gone over the entire room looking for the monster and it was not there.

They had a couple of cups of coffee and a couple of snifters of cognac as they waited to see if the monster would return but it didn't and their appreciation of Hawkline beauty increased some.

"Who painted that painting?" Cameron said.

"It was painted in France years ago," Miss Hawkline said.

"Whoever painted it sure knew how to paint," Cameron said, staring at the Hawkline sister who had just answered him. She liked the way Cameron was staring at her.

"Yes, the artist is very famous."

"Did you ever meet him?"

"No, he was dead years before I was born."

"That's a shame," Cameron said.

"Isn't it?" Miss Hawkline said.

# · Soliloquy of the Shadow ·

The Hawkline Monster had returned to its jar of chemicals in the laboratory. It lay there in repose . . . strange sections of light not moving. These chemicals, the long and arduous work of Professor Hawkline, were the energy source, rejuvenation and place where the Hawkline Monster slept when it was tired, and while the monster slept, The Chemicals restored its power.

The shadow of the Hawkline Monster slept nearby. The shadow was dreaming. It was dreaming that it was the monster and the monster was it. It was a very pleasant dream for the shadow.

The shadow liked the idea of not being the shadow anymore but instead being the monster itself. The shadow did not like to sneak around all the time. It made the shadow nervous and unhappy. The shadow often cursed its fate and wished that The Chemicals had given it a better throw of the dice.

In the shadow's dream it was the Hawkline Monster and occupying a bracelet on the wrist of one of the Hawkline sisters. It was very happy in the dream and trying to please her by making her bracelet shine more brightly.

The shadow did not approve of the monster's tactics and was ashamed of the cruel things that the monster had inflicted upon the minds of the Hawkline sisters. The shadow could not understand why the monster did these things. If fate were reversed and the shadow changed into the monster, everything would be different around the house. These cruel jokes would come to an end and the monster's energy would be directed to discovering and implementing new pleasures for the Hawkline sisters.

The shadow was very fond of them and hated to be a part of the monster's sense of humor and wished only pleasure and good times for the Hawkline sisters instead of the evil pranks that the monster loved to play upon their bodies and their minds.

The shadow also strongly disapproved of what the monster had done to Professor Hawkline. It thought that the monster should have been loyal to him and not pulled such a diabolical prank on him.

The bracelet dream of the shadow suddenly dispelled itself and the shadow was wide awake. It stared down at the Hawkline Monster sleeping in The Chemicals. For the first time, the shadow realized how much it hated the monster and tried to think of ways to end its evil existence and take the energy of The Chemicals and change them into good.

The monster slept unsuspecting in the jar of chemicals. The monster was tired from a day of evil deeds. It was so tired that it was snoring in The Chemicals.

# · Meanwhile, Back in the Parlor ·

It was now almost midnight and a Victorian clock was pushing Twentieth Century minutes toward twelve. Its ticking was loud and methodical as it devoured July 13, 1902.

Greer and Cameron casually but very carefully examined the parlor again to see if the Hawkline Monster had returned. It hadn't.

They of course did not know that it was sound asleep, snoring in a jar full of chemicals in the laboratory and they were all safe for the time being.

After they were certain that the monster was not about, Greer said to Cameron, "I think it's time we told them."

"Told us what?" Miss Hawkline said.

"About the monster," Greer said.

"What about it?" Miss Hawkline said.

Her sister had turned her attention from a cup of hot coffee in her hand to intently waiting for the next words from Greer.

Greer searched his mind to find the right words and a simple, logical sequence to tell them in. He paused a little too long because what he had to say was so fantastic that he could not easily find a simple way to say it. Finally the right words found him.

"The monster's not down in the ice caves," Greer said. "It's here in the house. It's been all over the place today. It spent a couple of hours sitting around your necks."

"What?" Miss Hawkline said, incredulously.

Her sister put her cup of coffee down.

They were both now in a state of amused shock.

"The monster's some kind of strange light that moves around followed by a goofy shadow," Greer said. "I don't know exactly how it works but it works and we're going to destroy it. We don't think there's anything in the ice caves that we've got to kill. The light has the power to change things and to think and it can get into minds and fuck 'em around. Have either of you noticed the light and the shadow that follows it like a dog?"

The Hawkline sisters did not say anything. They turned and stared at each other.

"Well?" Greer said.

Finally a Miss Hawkline spoke, "It's a strange light that moves around with a clumsy shadow following it?" she said.

"Yeah, we've seen it all over the place," Greer said. "It's been moving around with us, dogging us. For a long time this evening it was right there in your necklaces. It left a while ago and hasn't been back since."

"What you're describing is one of the properties of The Chemicals," Miss Hawkline said. "There's a strange light in the jar and a kind of swirly awkward shadow that stays near the light and follows it when it moves in the jar. The light is an advanced stage of The Chemicals. Our father told us before he disappeared that the light would eventually be changed into something that would be extremely beneficial for all mankind."

"We've needed some more chemicals to complete that change and those are the chemicals our poor butler brought us from Brooks. We were going to finish the experiment as soon as you killed the monster," the other Miss Hawkline said.

"I wouldn't finish anything," Greer said. "I think what you should do is to throw that batch of stuff out and start over again. You've got something that's out of control down there. I think that stuff killed your butler and is responsible for your father's disappearance and it also changed one of you girls into an Indian and has fucked with our minds, too."

The Hawkline sisters stared on, lost in deep silence.

"Let's go down and get that jar of fucking stuff and throw it out and then get a good night's sleep," Cameron said. "I could stand it. I've never buried a dwarf before and I'm tired. I've fucked so much today I'm afraid my prick's going to fall off."

"The Chemicals were our father's lifework," Miss Hawkline said, breaking silence desperately. "He dedicated his life to The Chemicals."

"We know that," Cameron said. "And we think the fucking chemicals turned on him. Bit the hand that fed them, so to speak. You saw what it did to your butler. It killed him and changed his body into a dwarf. The devil only knows what that fucking stuff is going to do next. We've got to throw it out before we're all changed into dead dwarfs. There's nobody to bury us in a bunch of suitcases."

# · Meanwhile, Back in the Jar ·

The Hawkline Monster, a light in a jar full of chemicals, slowly turned over like a sleeping person and then turned over again.

*God-damn it,* thought the shadow and slowly turned over and then turned over again.

The monster was now uncomfortable in its sleep and moved again like a person on the edge of waking up and turned over again and *God-damn it,* thought the shadow and turned over again.

The Hawkline Monster was uneasy in its sleep. Perhaps it was having a bad dream or a premonition. It turned over again and *God-damn it.*

# · A Man's Work Turned
# to Nothing ·

"You mean you want us to destroy our father's lifework?"
Miss Hawkline said.

"Yes," Cameron said. "It's either that or have it destroy
you."

"There has to be another alternative," the other Miss
Hawkline said. "We just can't throw away what he spent
twenty years working on."

It was a minute before the hour of midnight. Miss
Hawkline got up and put a lump of coal on the fire. The
other Miss Hawkline poured Greer some more coffee. She
was pouring from a silver coffee pot.

Everything had stopped momentarily while the Hawkline sisters were thinking about what to do next. It was an enormous decision for them to make.

"And don't forget we think that fucking thing got your father, too," Greer said, as the clock began tolling midnight and changing the world into July 14, 1902.

"4," Cameron said.

"Give us a few more minutes," Miss Hawkline said, looking anxiously over at her sister. "Just a few more minutes. We've got to make the right decision. Once it's done, it's done."

"OK," Greer said.

"12," Cameron said.

# · Waking Up ·

The Hawkline Monster continued stirring in The Chemicals. It was now almost awake. The shadow sighed as the monster hovered on the edge of waking. The shadow dreaded again being a part of the next thing the monster would think up. He did not approve of the way the monster fooled with the Hawkline women, making them do things that were completely out of character. The transformation of one Hawkline sister into an Indian, the shadow thought, was a very gross deed.

There was no way of knowing what the monster would come up with next. No thing was too terrible for the monster not to consider and of course its powers of dark invention had just barely been tapped.

The light which was the monster continued to toss and turn in The Chemicals as waking roared toward it like an early winter storm.

The shadow sighed again.

*God-damn it.*

Suddenly the monster was awake. It stopped stirring about and lay very quietly in The Chemicals. It looked over at the shadow. The shadow stared helplessly back, resigned to its fate.

The light looked away from the shadow. The light looked about the room. The light was anxious. It continued looking about the room, still a little sleepy but rapidly becoming energized. The light felt something threatening but it didn't know what it was.

Momentarily, it would be in full control of its powers.

The Hawkline Monster felt that something was very wrong.

The shadow watched its nervous master.

The monster's mind, like a tree in an early winter storm, shook off the leaves of sleep.

The shadow wished that the Hawkline Monster were dead, even though it would probably have to follow the monster into oblivion.

Anything was better than the living hell of having to be in partnership with the Hawkline Monster and do all these evil things.

The shadow remembered back to previous stages of The Chemicals and how exciting it was to be created by Professor Hawkline. At that time the light was benevolent, almost giddy with the excitement of having just been created. There was a future with the possibility of help and joy for all mankind. Then the light changed in attitude. The light concealed its personality change from Professor Hawkline.

The light started pulling little pranks that the professor let pass as accidents. Something falling over or something being changed into something else, so that the professor thought that he had made the mistake or something had been mislabeled and then the light found that it could leave the jar and move about and of course the poor innocent shadow of the light was forced to follow and become a participant-observer in pranks that gathered in momentum until they became acts of evil.

After while Professor Hawkline knew that there was something very wrong with The Chemicals but he kept thinking right up to the moment that the monster did that terrible thing to him that he would be able to correct the balance of The Chemicals and complete the experiment with humanitarian possibilities for the entire world.

But that was never to be because one afternoon when the professor was upstairs working on a new formula in his study the light pulled its most gross evil prank upon him.

The shadow shuddered to think about it.

The light was at last totally awake and knew that it was being severely threatened by the people upstairs and it had better take care of that threat right now.

The light crawled out of The Chemicals and balanced on the rim of the jar in preparation for departure and the shadow reluctantly prepared to follow.

# · The Decision ·

"Yes," Miss Hawkline said, finally.

Her sister nodded in agreement.

"It's a difficult decision but it's the only way," Miss Hawkline said. "I'm sorry that this had to happen to our father's lifework but there are things that are more important."

"Yeah, our lives," Cameron interrupted. He was impatient. He wanted to go downstairs right now and throw that jar of stuff out and then sleep tonight beside the body of a Hawkline woman. He was tired. It had been a long day.

"We have the formula to The Chemicals," Miss Hawkline said. "Perhaps we can start over again or give it to some-body who might be interested in it."

"I don't know," the other Miss Hawkline said. "I'm a little tired of the whole thing, so let's not talk about the future now. Let's just pour the stuff out and get some sleep. I'm tired."

"Those are my feelings," Cameron said.

# · Upstairs ·

The monster drifted off the lip of the jar and glided across the laboratory to land on the bottom step of the stairs that led upward to the house.

The shadow clumsily followed behind it, darker than the darkness in the room, more silent than complete silence and alone in the tragedy of its servitude to evil.

Then the Hawkline Monster flowed like a reverse waterfall up the stairs. It sparkled and reflected as it moved. The shadow followed behind it, a reluctant complement of darkness. The Hawkline Monster stopped at a dim space of light that shined under the laboratory door.

It was waiting for something to happen. The light of

the monster was now almost surgical in its perception. It looked under the door and down the hall.

The monster was anticipating something about to happen.

The shadow waited behind the Hawkline Monster. The shadow wished that it could look out underneath the door to see what was happening, but, alas, its role in life was only to follow and so it detailed itself right behind the ass of the Hawkline Monster.

# · Whiskey ·

Everybody started to leave the parlor to go downstairs and pour out the Hawkline Monster but just as they reached the door and one of the Hawkline women had her hand on the knob, Cameron said, "Hold it for a second. I want to get myself a little whiskey." He walked over to the table where the liquor was in various cut-glass decanters.

He paused, trying to figure out which bottle was the whiskey. Then one of the Hawkline sisters said, "It's the bottle with the blue top."

That Miss Hawkline was carrying a lamp.

Cameron took a glass and poured himself a big slug of whiskey. Greer thought that this was strange because

Cameron never took a drop before a job and certainly the destruction of the monster was a job.

Cameron held the glass of whiskey up to his nose. "Sure smells like the good stuff."

Greer in sudden anticipation of killing the monster did not notice that Cameron, though he had poured himself a big glass of whiskey, did not take a drink from it. When they left the room, he was carrying the glass in his hand.

# · Searching for a Container ·

Then a parlor door opened to the hall and one of the Hawkline sisters stepped into the hall, followed by another sister
and Greer and Cameron who had a glass of whiskey in his
hand.

 The shadow could not see over the Hawkline Monster
but the shadow heard the door opening and the people coming out into the hall. It wondered what was up, why the
monster was so interested in the people at this time. Then
the shadow shrugged. It was useless to continue with this
line of thought for there was nothing that the shadow could
do about it. The shadow could only follow the Hawkline
Monster which it hated.

The Hawkline Monster watched them come down the hall toward the laboratory door. It waited, contemplating what form of action to follow next. It tried to realize a container, a shape to put its magic and its spells in and then to evoke that container upon these people who threatened its existence.

The shadow by now had given up trying to figure out what was happening. The shadow just didn't give a fuck anymore.

# · To Kill a Jar ·

"Do you think we need a gun?" Greer said to Cameron.

There was no reply.

Greer thought that perhaps Cameron hadn't heard him, so he repeated the question.

"To kill a jar?" Cameron said.

The Hawkline women smiled.

Greer did not get the joke. He also did not notice that Cameron still had the glass of whiskey in his hand. Greer was unusually excited by the prospect of direct confrontation with the Hawkline Monster.

Cameron was carrying the glass of whiskey the same way he carried a pistol, casual but professional, waiting to be supereffective without any impression of menace.

Even the monster watching from underneath the laboratory door paid no attention to the glass of whiskey in Cameron's hand.

The Hawkline Monster had by now formulated a plan to take care of the threat to its life. The monster smiled at its own cunning. It liked the plan because it was so fiendish.

The monster suddenly backed its ass up and moved down a step toward the laboratory floor and knocked the unsuspecting shadow down two steps.

*Fuck!* the shadow thought and tried to regain some of its nonexistent dignity while keeping a close watch now on the Hawkline Monster, so that it could follow what the monster did next because that is the business of shadows.

# · The Elephant Foot
# Umbrella Stand ·

As they walked down the hall, they passed the elephant foot umbrella stand and Cameron could not but count the umbrellas in the stand.

. . . 7, 8, 9.

Nine umbrellas.

Miss Hawkline paused beside the stand. There was something very familiar about it but she could not figure out what it was. There was just something very familiar. She wondered what it was.

"What is it?" Greer said.

Miss Hawkline was standing there staring at the umbrella stand. She thought that she had paused there for just a few seconds but it was longer than that and she did not realize it because she was lost in total curiosity.

She was holding up the possible demise of the Hawkline Monster.

"This elephant foot umbrella stand is very familiar," she said, addressing her sister. "Is it familiar to you?"

Her sister, who was also Miss Hawkline, took a look at it. Her gaze was suddenly equally intent. "Yes, it is familiar but I don't know what it is about it that is familiar. It almost reminds me of a person but I can't quite figure out who it is. It's somebody I've met, though."

Greer and Cameron looked at each other and then carefully around the hall. They were looking for the monster but they didn't see it. This conversation about the elephant foot umbrella stand had all the markings of the kind of stuff the monster would pull off.

But the monster was nowhere in sight, so they mentally put aside this Hawkline sister concentration as mere eccentricity.

"It certainly does remind me of somebody," Miss Hawkline said.

"Why don't you think about it later after we've finished off the monster? There'll be plenty of time for you to figure out who it is, then," Cameron said.

# · The Hawkline Monster
## in 4/4 Beat ·

The Hawkline Monster backed down the stairs to the laboratory, causing a shimmering flow of light like an ungodly waterfall. It also caused a confused inept shadow to bungle along in front of it.

The Hawkline Monster was now very confident. It knew how to handle things and looked forward in anticipation to the results of its power.

The Hawkline Monster had conceived of a diabolical fate for Greer, Cameron and the Hawkline women. It considered the plan one of the best things that it had ever come up with. It was the true amalgamation of mischief and evil.

The Hawkline Monster almost laughed as it strategically retreated down into the laboratory with its shadow scrambling awkwardly, tumbling goofily and carrying on in a demeaning, laughable manner as it tried to perform the perfunctory tasks of a shadow.

The Hawkline Monster was basking in confidence as it drifted and flowed down the stairs. What did it need to worry about because after all, did it not have the power to change objects and thoughts into whatever form amused it?

# · Daddy ·

Miss Hawkline opened the iron door to the laboratory. She pulled back the two bolts and took the key from her pocket which soon released the huge padlock. All the time that she was opening the door, her mind was fixed on the elephant foot umbrella stand trying to figure out what person it reminded her of. The recognition of that person hovered right on the edge of her mind.

She pulled back the first bolt on the door. It was a little hard to get back, so she had to give it a good tug.

That umbrella stand was so familiar.

*Who was it?*

She pulled back the second bolt. It came back much easier than the first one did. She barely had to pull on it.

*I've seen that umbrella stand thousands of times before but not as an umbrella stand,* she thought, *but as somebody I know.*

She took a large key from the pocket of her dress and inserted the key into the huge padlock on the door and she turned the key and the lock fell open like a clenched fist and she took the lock off the door and hung it on the hasp.

Then she yelled, "DADDY!" and turned and ran down the hall to the elephant foot umbrella stand.

# · A Harem of Shadows ·

The Hawkline Monster had found itself a good position of concealment in the laboratory and now just waited for Greer, Cameron and the Hawkline women to come into its domain.

The Hawkline Monster was so confident of their future that it was not even curious when it heard one of the Hawkline sisters scream and run back down the hall away from the laboratory door, followed by everybody else.

What difference did it make what they did up there for soon they would return and come down that flight of stairs and the Hawkline Monster would play with them a little bit. Then it would change them all into shadows and the monster would have five shadows following after it instead of one incompetent shadow.

Perhaps, these four new shadows would be skillful at playing the role the Hawkline Monster had devised for them. *Yes,* the monster thought, *it could stand a little competence in the shadow line.*

The Hawkline Monster had concealed itself behind some test tubes full of chemicals which were a rejected possibility of de-eviling The Chemicals that the professor had worked on for months before abandoning them as failures.

The shadow had concealed itself behind a clock on the table beside the test tubes. As soon as there was light in the laboratory the incompetence of its concealment would be revealed.

The shadow could not do anything right.

"Soon you will have playmates," the Hawkline Monster said to the shadow.

The shadow didn't know what the fuck the Hawkline Monster was talking about.

# · Father and Daughters Reunited (Sort of ·

Miss Hawkline was on her knees and she had thrown her arms around the elephant foot umbrella stand and she was sobbing uncontrollably and saying over and over again, "Daddy! Daddy!"

The other Miss Hawkline stood there looking down at her sister, trying to figure out what was happening.

Greer and Cameron were busy looking around for the Hawkline Monster. Had they missed seeing it when they had looked for it before? Or had it come up behind them in the hall? They looked all over but they couldn't find the monster anywhere.

Then the other Miss Hawkline bent forward and looked very hard at the elephant foot umbrella stand.

Suddenly a huge flash of emotion exploded itself across her face and she fell to her knees beside her sister and said, "Oh, Father! It's our father! Daddy!"

The Hawkline sisters were not as emotionless as they thought they were.

Greer and Cameron stood there watching the Hawkline sisters hugging and calling an elephant foot umbrella stand Daddy.

# · Marriage ·

Greer and Cameron left the Hawkline women with the elephant foot umbrella stand and walked back down the hall to the laboratory door. It was time to do something about the Hawkline Monster and right now. Greer and Cameron had had enough of its antics.

Greer was now carrying the lamp.

Cameron had a glass of whiskey in his hand.

Greer still had not noticed anything different about Cameron carrying the glass of whiskey. His mind was really someplace else because under any other conditions, he would have noticed the glass of whiskey. This was a first for him. Perhaps it was time that he should start thinking about retiring, about hanging it up and finding a good woman to settle down with.

Yes, that was probably a good idea. Maybe one of the Hawkline women. He of course had no way of knowing that the Hawkline Monster had already planned a sort of group marriage for them, anyway.

# · Dream Residence ·

Greer went first. He opened the laboratory door and the light from the lamp in his hand illuminated the stairs and part of the laboratory. It was a very complicated place. Greer had never seen anything like it before. There were tables covered with thousands of bottles. There were machines that would have been at home in a dream.

"Go on, Greer. Let's go down and look around," Cameron said.

"OK."

The Hawkline Monster was watching them. The monster was amused by their helplessness. The women were not with them but the monster would take care of them after it had finished with Greer and Cameron. There was plenty of time for everybody.

The monster was so gleeful about the horrors that it was about to perform that it did not notice that a strangeness was being generated inside the shadow.

The shadow had been watching Greer and Cameron as they came down the stairs and then went over and lit three or four lamps, so they could see better, but then the shadow turned its attention to the Hawkline Monster and was staring at it and a strange for-the-first-time feeling was being born in the shadow as it continued to stare harder and harder at the Hawkline Monster.

A unique thought was now in the shadow's mind and the thought was linking itself up with a plan of direct action to take place when next the monster chose to move.

"This sure is a weird place," Greer said.

"It ain't any weirder than Hawaii," Cameron said.

# · The Battle ·

Cameron had spotted the hiding place of the Hawkline Monster when he and Greer were halfway down the stairs. He saw strange sparks of light on a bench behind some funny-looking bottles. He didn't know what a test tube was.

"Why don't you light those lamps over there?" he said, motioning Greer over to a bench on the far side of the laboratory.

The Hawkline Monster was amused as it watched them. The monster was deriving so much pleasure from this that it decided to wait a few minutes before changing Greer and Cameron into shadows.

This was real fun for the monster.

Meanwhile, its current and only shadow waited for the monster to move so that it could put into action a plan of its own.

Cameron had also spotted a large leaded-crystal jar on a table in the opposite direction that he had sent Greer to light some lamps.

From the description that the Hawkline women had given him, he knew that this was the source of the Hawkline Monster . . . The Chemicals. He was standing about ten feet away from the jar. And the monster was "hiding" about five feet away from the jar.

Suddenly Cameron yelled, "It's over there! I see it!"

Greer turned toward where Cameron was yelling and pointing. He couldn't figure out what was happening. Why Cameron was yelling. This was not like Cameron but he turned anyway to the direction.

The Hawkline Monster was curious, too. What in the hell was happening? What was over there if it was over here?

So the monster moved . . . involuntarily . . . out of curiosity.

Cameron in the interim of artificial excitement moved over to the table where a jar called The Chemicals was residing and he was standing right beside it.

When the Hawkline Monster moved to get a better view of what was happening, the shadow, after having checked all the possibilities of light, had discovered a way that it could shift itself in front of the monster, so that the monster at this crucial time would be blinded by darkness for a few seconds, did so, causing confusion to befall the monster.

This was all that the shadow could do and it hoped that

this would give Greer and Cameron the edge they would need to destroy the Hawkline Monster using whatever plan they had come up with, for it seemed that they must have a plan if they were to have any chance at all with the monster and they did not seem like fools.

When Cameron yelled at Greer, the shadow interpreted this as the time to move and did so. It obscured the vision of the Hawkline Monster for a few seconds, knowing full well that if the monster were destroyed it would be destroyed, too, but death was better than going on living like this, being a part of this evil.

The Hawkline Monster raged against the shadow, trying to get it out of the way, so that it could see what was happening.

But the shadow struggled fiercely with the monster. The shadow had a burst of unbelievable physical fury and shadows are not known for their strength.

# · The Passing of the Hawkline Monster ·

Cameron poured the glass of whiskey into the jar of chemicals. When the whiskey hit The Chemicals they turned blue and started bubbling and sparks began flying from the jar. The sparks were like small birds of fire and flew about burning everything they touched.

"Let's get out of here!" Cameron yelled at Greer. They both fled up the laboratory stairs to the main floor of the house.

The Hawkline Monster responded to the whiskey being poured into the jar of its energy source by just having enough time to curse its fate

"FUCK IT!"

the monster yelled. It was a classic curse before shattering into a handful of blue diamonds that had no memory of a previous existence.

The Hawkline Monster was nothing now except diamonds. They sparkled like a vision of summer sky. The shadow of the monster had been turned into the shadow of diamonds. It also was without memory of a previous existence, so now its soul was at rest and it had been turned into the shadow of beautiful things.

# · The Return of Professor Hawkline ·

Greer and Cameron rushed up out of the burning laboratory and down the hall toward the Hawkline sisters. Just then the elephant foot umbrella stand changed into Professor Hawkline. He had been held prisoner in that form by a spell from the just-freshly-defunct Hawkline Monster who would now be at home in a jewelry store window.

Professor Hawkline was stiff and cranky from having spent long months as an umbrella stand. He wasn't as friendly to his loving daughters as he should have been, for the first words that came from his mouth in direct response to their cooing, "Daddy, Daddy. It's you. You're free. Father. Oh, Daddy," were, "Oh, shit!"

He didn't have time to say anything else before Greer and Cameron were upon him and his two daughters and hustling them out of the burning house.

# · The Lazarus Dynamic ·

When they got outside they ran to just beyond the frost that encircled the burning house like a transparent wedding ring.

A few moments later they were all carefully watching the fire when suddenly the ground near them began to rumble and move like a small earthquake.

It was coming from the butler's grave.

"What the hell!" Greer said.

Then the ground opened up and out popped the butler like a giant mole covered with dirt and there were bits and pieces of a suitcase lying around him.

"Where . . . Am . . . I?" rumbled his deep old voice.

He was trying to shake the dirt off his arms and shoulders. He was very confused. He had never been buried before.

"You just came back from the dead," Cameron said as he turned back to watch the house burning down.

# · An Early Twentieth-
# Century Picnic ·

They stood there for a long time watching the house burn down. The flames roared high into the sky. They were so bright that everybody had shadows.

The professor had by now returned to a normal disposition and he had his arms affectionately around his daughters as they watched the house go.

"That was quite a batch of stuff you mixed up there, Professor," Cameron said.

"Never again," was the professor's response.

He had been introduced to Greer and Cameron and he liked them and was very grateful for their having rescued him from the curse of The Chemicals which could also be called the Hawkline Monster.

Eventually they just sat down on the ground and watched the house burn all night long. It kept them warm. The Hawkline sisters changed the loving arms of their father for the arms of Greer and Cameron. The professor sat by himself contemplating the result of all his years of experimenting and how it had led to this conclusion.

From time to time he would shake his head but he was also very glad not to be an elephant foot umbrella stand any more. That was the worst experience he'd ever had in his life.

The butler was sitting there still dumbfounded and brushing the dirt off his clothes. There was a piece of suitcase in his hair.

The way everybody was sitting it looked as if they were at a picnic but the picnic was of course the burning of a house, the death of the Hawkline Monster and the end of a scientific dream. It was barely the Twentieth Century.

# · The Hawkline Diamonds ·

By the light of the morning sun the house was gone and in its place was a small lake floating with burned things. Everybody got up off the ground and walked down to the shores of the new lake.

The Hawklines looked at the remnants of their previous life floating here and there on the lake. Professor Hawkline saw part of an umbrella and shuddered.

One of the Hawkline women noticed what had disturbed her father and reached over and took his hand. "Look, Susan," she said to her sister and then pointed at a photograph floating out there.

Greer and Cameron looked at each other.

Susan!

"Yes, Jane," was the reply.

Jane!

The Hawkline women had first names and another prank of that damn ingenious monster had been dispelled.

Some of the house was still smoldering at the edge of the lake. It looked very strange. It was almost like something out of Hieronymus Bosch if he had been into Western landscapes.

"I'm curious," Cameron said. "I'm going to dive down into the basement and see if there's anything left of that fucking monster."

He took his clothes off down to a pair of shorts and dove into what just a few hours before had been a house. He was a good swimmer and swam easily down into the basement and started looking around for the monster. He remembered where the monster had been hiding before he poured the whiskey into The Chemicals.

He swam over there and found a handful of blue diamonds lying on the floor. The monster was nowhere in sight. The diamonds were very beautiful. He gathered them all together in his hand and swam upward out of the laboratory to the shore of the lake which had once been a front porch.

"Look," he said, climbing up onto the bank. Everybody gathered around and admired the diamonds. Cameron was holding them in such a way as for there to be a shadow. The shadow of the diamonds was beautiful, too.

"We're rich," Cameron said.

"We're already rich," Professor Hawkline said. The Hawkline family was a very rich family in its own right.

"Oh," Cameron said.

"You mean, you're rich," Susan Hawkline said, but you still couldn't tell the difference between her and her sister Jane. So actually the name-stealing curse of the Hawkline Monster really hadn't made that much difference, anyway.

"What about the monster?" Professor Hawkline said.

"No, it's destroyed. When I poured that glass of whiskey in The Chemicals, that did it."

"Yeah, it burned my house down," Professor Hawkline said, suddenly remembering that he no longer had a house. He liked that house. It had contained the best laboratory he'd ever had and he thought that the ice caves made a good conversation piece.

His voice sounded a little bitter.

"Would you like to be an elephant foot umbrella stand again?" Greer said, checking in with his arm around a Hawkline woman.

"No," the professor said.

"What are we going to do now?" Susan Hawkline said, surveying the lake that had once been their house.

Cameron counted the diamonds in his hand. There were thirty-five diamonds and they were all that was left of the Hawkline Monster.

"We'll think of something," Cameron said.

# · Lake Hawkline ·

Somehow the burning of the house caused the ice caves to melt even down to their deepest recesses and the site of the former house became a permanent lake.

In 1907 William Langford, a local rancher, purchased the property from Professor Hawkline who had been living *back* East ever since his strange sojourn in the West.

The professor had given up chemistry and was now devoting his life to stamp collecting.

William Langford used the lake for irrigation and had a nice farm around it, mostly potatoes.

Professor Hawkline had been so glad to get rid of the property that he sold it for half of what it was worth but that didn't make any difference to him because he was happy to get rid of the place. It had a lot of bad elephant foot umbrella stand memories for him.

He never went West again.

And what happened to everybody else?

Well, it went something like this:

Greer and Jane Hawkline moved to Butte, Montana, where they started a whorehouse. They got married but were divorced in 1906. Jane Hawkline ended up with possession of the whorehouse and ran it until 1911 when she was killed in an automobile accident.

The accident had barely killed her and she was quite beautiful in death. The funeral was enjoyed and remembered by all who attended.

Greer was arrested for auto theft in 1927 and spent four years in the Wyoming State Penitentiary where he developed an interest in the Rosicrucian way of faith.

Cameron and Susan Hawkline were going to get married but they got into a huge argument about Cameron counting things all the time and Susan Hawkline left Portland, Oregon, in a huff and went to Paris, France, where she married a Russian count and moved to Moscow. She was killed by a stray bullet during the Russian Revolution in October 1917.

The diamonds that had formerly been the Hawkline Monster?

Spent long ago. Scattered over the world. Lost.

The shadow of the Hawkline Monster?

With the diamonds and blessedly without memory of previous times.

As for Cameron, he eventually became a successful movie producer in Hollywood, California, during the boom period just before World War I. How he became a movie producer is a long and complicated story that should be saved for another time.

In 1928 William Langford's heirs sold Lake Hawkline and the surrounding property to the State of Oregon that turned it into a park but being in a fairly remote area of Oregon with very poor roads, the lake never developed into a popular recreational site and doesn't get many visitors.